SINISTER STREET

Curated by D.L. Winchester,
Edited by Tasha Schiedel

CONTENTS

SINISTER STREET

COFFEE, TOAST, GARDEN

BY MATTHEW R DAVIS

COFFEE, TOAST, GARDEN

BY MATTHEW R. DAVIS

Delia had been making plans for the garden even before she and Gustavo finalised their purchase of the house on Dowling Street, but the first month there was eaten up by a slew of other tasks—unpacking separate lives from a never-ending series of boxes, bargaining over whose furniture went where, arranging a cleaning schedule around his fly-in, fly-out roster of two weeks away and one week home—and even with her days now free of work-imposed structure, she always seemed to find more and more things that needed doing. At the start of the second month, with Gustavo's side of the bed over a week cold and another five days before his flight home from the mining village, Delia fixed herself a strong coffee, tucked her camellia-pink hair under a sunhat, and finally headed out into the back yard to make those plans a reality.

First thing on the list was getting rid of all those pots. When the house had been built forty-odd years prior, someone had apparently bought a lot of plants and left them to stand around half-buried in their black plastic buckets come what may. The yard had swallowed these pots over the ensuing decades as earth built up around them, and now Delia saw their dark lips poking out of the dirt at every turn like the lids of haphazardly buried coffins. Agaves, touch-me-nots, jade trees, lilly pillies, even the twenty-foot palm dominating the lawn that had been placed irritatingly off-centre—each had grown in, through, and out of a plastic pot, and Delia did not intend to spend the rest of her life staring at such sloppy work.

She began in the back left corner of the yard, shaded by a giant Moreton Bay fig tree as her shovel bit into the earth around a series of jade plants that had grown horizontally from tilted pots. No sooner had she removed these, planning to sell them online to make the effort financially worthwhile, than her blade hit something deeper in the soil. Delia uncovered more pots, these empty and pointless, and dug them out with a resigned grimace. Turning over the earth, her shovel scraped against something harder, harsher. She brushed the dirt clear with one gloved hand and discovered a cement border buried a foot below the surface. Pulling out her phone, she messaged Gustavo.

Last owner probably didn't even bother clearing the block. Just dumped some dirt on it, chucked potted plants at it & let it go. UGH.

A moment later, her phone buzzed.

Own it, D. Go crazy!

Another hour's work uncovered a good two metres of the cement border, which Delia assumed had lined an older garden bed that predated the brick house she now called home. She brushed it clear to see if it was worth reusing and found the cement had been carved with a sequence of symbols, stars and suns and moons. The work was intricate, a labour of love. Delia had never seen such a thing and assumed the inscriptions had been painstakingly undertaken by the previous occupant.

> *At least SOMEONE once cared how this garden looked… Looking forward to having you home again and in my arms. x*

By the end of her first day, Delia had excavated ten pots and a smattering of minor finds: three one-cent coins minted in the 1970s, five shards of frosted glass, six small bones she could not identify. She hung up her shovel and counted the day a worthy one, ate a small dinner, relaxed in the bath with a gruesome paperback. This last was one of the few things she had carried over from living with her mother, a rare positive legacy from Della Clough. Towelling off afterward, Delia eyed herself in the mirror and decided that the pink in her hair had faded enough to warrant a replacement—a little too much of that distinctive Clough ash-blonde was peeking through at the roots. She left a tube of lobelia-blue dye out on the sink to remind herself and wound down her night.

> *See you soon, D. Looking forward to seeing ALL of you. ;)*

Delia woke early the next morning, sure that she'd heard someone knocking at the back door. Realising this was highly unlikely, she rolled over and stretched, enjoying the tenderness in her muscles from the previous day's workout. Coffee, toast, and she was out in the garden in her grubbies again, digging her way along the back fence and uprooting some ugly succulents she was keen to replace. That buried cement border ran all the way along, a metre inside the fence line, and she brushed it clear as she went, uncovering more carvings. The sigils became less familiar, more abstract; she assumed they were still astronomical in theme, but their meaning eluded her.

Between two potted agaves, Delia found another strange remnant. Someone had buried the cement bowl of a birdbath, or perhaps it too had simply been ploughed over when her house had been built and its slapdash garden installed. Presumably it had been kept out here for its intended purpose, though she found another carving in its centre: a stylised eye that she first took to be an Egyptian hieroglyph until she realised it bore two pupils, growing from each other like codependent peas in a pod. She imagined it as a mystical security system keeping watch on visiting birds as they drank, but the whimsy didn't make it any less disturbing.

Before she knew it, the sun had crossed the midpoint of the sky and her stomach was reminding her of certain obligations. Delia broke for lunch, munching on a carrot and cheese sandwich as she sat against the back wall of the house and admired the progress she'd made. She imagined sweet Gustavo's delight at how industrious she'd been. Too often lately she'd been feeling listless and unproductive, guiltily watching him lug furniture into place as he refused her help and insisted that she take it easy. What was she, delicate china to be preserved? She was already plenty chipped. A decade and a half with her mother had made sure of that.

Brushing old thoughts aside, Delia bent over her shovel once more. It stabbed into the earth like a knife into a body, and more than once, she worried that she was murdering the yard, that Gustavo would come home and wonder why she'd decided to mutilate a perfectly fine garden. Surely he understood that some things *needed* to be changed, removed from past contexts and made fresh—the way she had painstakingly recast herself as a sane and likeable woman instead of the neurotic, hair-chewing high-schooler dismissed by her peers as Psycho Delia, *sane* and *likeable* being two traits her mother had never been accused of with any accuracy.

Late afternoon found her leaning on her tool like a weary farmer, staring at the day's work. The back end of the garden was now a trench, two feet lower than the rest of the yard, and the carved cement border ran all along that depression like the exposed spine of a dinosaur skeleton. She'd found other bones, too, most of them too big to fit her previous theory that they were the remnants of decades-old dog meals; some of them were large enough that they might have come from dogs themselves. Delia imagined uncovering a leering canine skull and shuddered. Some things should remain buried. Some secrets the soil should keep close forever.

Soup and a roll for dinner, and then into the bathroom to redo her hair. Her re-emerging natural colour disappeared under a slathering of new blue, heredity denied for another month. Chatty colleagues at her last job had wondered why she continued to pollute such lovely ash-blonde hair, but then, they had understood so little about her. If they had been a little more accepting and less critical, perhaps the breakdown wouldn't have happened; perhaps she would still be working there. But she was not, and while her new colour set, she opened her laptop to find out more about the property she now called home.

Basic information on the house was easy to come by: it had been built in 1979 during a period of suburban growth and only sold the once, to she and Gustavo, for an eye-watering sum compared to the going rate just five years before. Delia already knew the name of the woman who had lived here in the interim, only moving into a nursing home once her husband had died and her own health had declined past the point of personal autonomy—knew that Benita Carlsberg had passed away the year before, prompting her daughter to put the house on the market at last. It was safe to assume the garden had been redone shortly after construction, but how had it looked prior to that? And what kind of home had it first attended? Here, her rudimentary Google-fu failed her. She put her questions aside for the moment and messaged Gustavo, who, due to the time differential between the southern and western coasts, had just hit his mid-shift break.

Delia dreamed again that someone was knocking at her back door, only when she went to investigate, she found herself standing in the kitchen of her mother's house. Della Clough shot her a wicked smile, bridged her crimson lips with one warning finger, then opened the door. Darkness swarmed in, and Delia opened her eyes to the morning sun.

She got up and got on with her day, keen to shake bitter old memories. Coffee, toast, garden. She gripped her shovel with blistered hands and worked her way along the left-hand fence, tearing out plants she knew to be mildly poisonous and heaping them together for the organics bin, stacking another dozen dirty pots along the back wall. She cleared off a space she'd marked for a row of rose bushes, paused for a breather and a drink of water. Then she tackled the right-hand fence, finding that the cement edging carried on all around the yard. Its carvings were so obscure now as to be meaningless to her, but maybe time had eroded simple symbols into incoherence, or perhaps their import was more esoteric. The previous garden would date back to the Sixties at least, so the first house's owner could've been on some real hippie trip; maybe she'd brought much older beliefs and practices into her work. Delia assumed the gardener had been a woman, could almost get a sense of her as she plunged her shovel into the soil time and again. That sense took a dark turn when she uncovered the sundered body.

She'd already dug up another slew of bones, each one bigger and less familiar than the last, but this was the first piece of statuary. Or rather, the first two pieces: a little girl in a shepherdess dress, one hand clutching a crook and the other a bunch of carven flowers, her neck ending in a strangely smooth stump; and a woman's head that must have come from another statue entirely, too large for the girl's body, its face worked into a smirk that was entirely and distastefully adult. Delia shuddered as a personal connection thumped into place, and when she moved the statuary to the back wall along with her growing collection of unearthed pots, she made sure that smug woman's head was kept a safe distance from the girl's innocent body. She felt an urge to take her shovel and smash the sly face into pieces, so strong that a spell of dizziness left her leaning on the haft of her spade. The gloom didn't lift when she recovered her wits, and she realised the sun was almost entirely down. She'd spent the whole afternoon at work without a single thought to water or rest.

Dazzled by the intensity of her labours, Delia retired inside and ran herself a bath. She found herself too distracted to concentrate on the paperback, and the water seemed to cool to an uncomfortable chill faster than usual. She dried off, slipped into pajamas, and ensconced herself on the couch, surrounded by small comforts: Lana Del Rey songs, dark chocolate, and a resolve to learn more about the place where she'd now be spending most, if not all, of the rest of her life. But she found her mind constantly paging back to that stone head, its knowing grin, and found she could avoid the unpleasant parallel no longer. After all, she'd already dreamed of it this morning.

Della Clough had embodied many faults, not least a habitual disdain for motherly love and positive reinforcement, and one of the most glaring was her infidelity. Delia's father had been that most clichéd of cuckolds, a neat and dull accountant whose household vocabulary had gradually worn down to *yes, dear* and *no, dear*, and he spent the weekday hours between eight and six out of the home. Many a time, when school holidays rolled around and sad little Psycho Delia found herself friendless and confined to the house, she'd heard a knocking at the back door and known that it was happening again—Della opening up to a gentleman caller, her grinning lips slicked red with stick-blood, her sharp eyes cutting a warning to her difficult daughter: *make yourself scarce and don't you dare say a word*. That was possibly the most enduring memory Delia had of her mother: standing by the kitchen door in a halter-neck satin dress more pungently glamorous than anything she wore in public, her ash-blonde hair pulled free of its usual confinement to hang loose in a fragrant curtain, her face thrumming with unspoken threats to her child even as it glowed with sly delight at the bedroom-bound hour to come.

She sounds like a real bitch, Gustavo had once said of Della, as ignorant of these infidelities as Delia's father had been and yet easily parsing the woman's nature from what little his partner chose to share. *Everything had to be all about her, didn't it? I mean, even your name... I'm sorry she's dead, D, but you deserved so much better.*

And she did—she had always known that, even if she'd not been able to say it aloud when the woman was still around. Sometimes it felt to Delia as though her whole life had been a struggle not to turn out like her mother, from the regular dyeing of her hair to her conscious kindness and refusal to openly judge. Whilst she'd never been able to confess Della's betrayals to her father during the short span of his widowerhood, she tried to make up for the woman's failings by always considering him, caring for him as he ailed and dutifully followed his faithless wife into a grave as cold and silent as the bed they'd shared. In her darkest moments, Delia couldn't help but imagine her mother's bitter words worming through the dirt between their coffins, allowing her husband no rest even in death.

> *Thinking of you, sweetheart. Not long to go now! xxx*

Gustavo's message broke her free of maundering thoughts. She sent a kiss back and turned her attention to the laptop. She tried and failed to access council records, looking for news articles in past decades that might have mentioned the place before her own. After an hour of fruitless searching, she remembered the recherché carvings on the garden's old cement border and amused herself by typing in *dowling street witch house*. And at last, she hit upon a promising entry.

The blog post was by a local amateur writer and musician who called herself Coffineyes. It dated from five years past and went by the title of *That House Where No-one Dares Go*. Not exactly primo reportage, but Delia clicked on it nonetheless.

My mother grew up on Dowling Street and—have you heard this one, too?—there was that house where no-one dared go. An old lady lived there alone, and of course, all the kids thought she was a witch. Mum never even saw her as she was just a little girl back then, but that just made it more believable—there was no inconvenient evidence to the contrary. I mean, she was probably just a lonely lady who'd lost her life's love or never wanted one to start with, but the way Mum heard it, she was the dark heart of the neighbourhood... or maybe the festering cancer.

So what did this woman do? Nothing! No-one saw more of her than a dim figure watering her garden at night, and no-one spoke to her except for the occasional stranger who turned up on her doorstep and spent a mysterious hour inside. No-one local dared to knock on her door, only charity collectors and God-botherers. Most of them were ignored... but there was a story about one young census-taker who was allowed an audience, who saw what lay inside that house.

What happened then is surely just an urban myth—we've all heard those tall tales that seem to spawn from some anonymous source, no-one ever taking credit for them—but rumour had it that the woman fled that place in terror. Mum even heard it said that her hair turned white, but that's obviously nonsense. It probably never happened at all. Kids' lives are full of bogus stories, ones they're fed and ones they make up to cope. We all have our mechanisms for dealing with life, and fiction is one of the least harmful.

No-one burned the witch. No-one even knew what happened to her in the end. Mum said that the neighbours noticed her mail piling up, her garden wilting in the sun, and eventually someone called the cops to check on her. They received no reply and forced their way in. Shortly, an ambulance came, and the woman finally left her house... under a sheet. People whispered that the police found strange things inside, things they refused to speak about. It was rumoured that some of those officers later quit to take up drinking instead. More nonsense, no doubt! But it's true that the house was demolished with unseemly haste, the block built over with a new home by people who made sure they were seen to be neighbourly. Does anything of the old lady linger there still? Or has her weirdness been blanded out of existence by suburban mundanity?

I know which I'd prefer. But if you've been reading my blog, you know what I like and how I think. Speaking of which, I put a new song up this week. Let me know what you think, freakers!

Winks and wonders,

Coffineyes

Delia mused over the entry, parsing out what little substance it held, and then she clicked on the link at the bottom of the blog. It transported her to a Bandcamp page, where Coffineyes had posted a dozen releases over the years. The genre was witch house, which was no doubt what had drawn Google's attention, and it seemed to be some subgenre of goth electronica. Delia spent the next hour sampling the woman's catalogue, at first because she felt she owed Coffineyes a few plays in return for the post, then because she found a strange comfort in its chopped beats, mutilated synths, and distorted vocals. She even bookmarked the page for later, grinning at the thought of Gustavo's reaction to these grim chants and horror-movie vibes.

Wearier than ever, she sloped off to bed and lay in the dark, thinking over what she'd read. Could it be that the woman who'd lived on this block before Benita Carlsberg *had* been a witch, or was Delia merely sunstruck and suggestible, eager to find meaning in even the vaguest of tales? She'd never believed in occult matters, so surely any implications in that direction were as empty of substance as her parents' marriage. She flicked through a few of her favourite photos of Gustavo and sent him a last message before putting her phone down and turning over into a swift, deep sleep.

> *I love you, my charming gentleman. Goodnight. x*

She didn't dream of anyone knocking at the back door this time, though she did find herself standing in a darkened kitchen, shivering at the sharp-edged echoes of her mother's hungry-hyena laugh. Other sounds reverberated through the dimness around her, things she'd had to endure after Della had retired to her room with her unseen callers, sighs and cries that were nothing like the discreet huffing she'd accidentally overheard once or twice when her parents were in bed together. The laughter increased in volume, slashing through the black like a razorblade smile and cutting open a door with a flapping of flensed flesh, and Delia was awake once more.

Three straight days of hard toil had left her weakened, blistered, and sore, but she rolled out of bed and went through her routine anyway. She scowled into her bathroom mirror when she saw that the lobelia-blue seemed to be fading already, receding from her roots as though her natural shade were keen to reassert itself. She tucked her hair under her sunhat and headed out into the yard, picked up the shovel with her nitrile-coated nylon gauntlets like a warrior taking up her blade for an oncoming battle. The trench awaited, lined with the long-buried cement verge, but there seemed nothing more she could uncover there. She started off in the almost-centre of the back lawn, where the tall palm sat with its many arms spread amid curls of long-broken pot, attended by a clutch of other plants that had failed to escape their own confines.

The sun was directly overhead when she came back to herself and found the palm standing alone in a ring of bare soil, the sole survivor of a struggle that had left the earth excavated to a depth of over a foot. That battle seemed comprehensively won, so she turned away from the carnage and found herself staring at the rear wall of her house. It looked so bare with only a window to break up the static brick pattern; no back door presented itself to be knocked upon, but perhaps the old place had boasted one. What other features might it have worn, and did any sign remain? Delia slurped some water, then stumbled to the edge of the lawn and began hacking mechanically at the dirt there. The floppy rim of her hat blocked out the sun and she heard nothing but the eager bite of her spade, the panting of desperate breath that cast her back into torrid holiday afternoons she could never seem to escape.

Delia was startled into full awareness when her rump crashed into the dirt, and she clutched at the earth beneath her with aching fingers as she fought off a spell of dizziness. Everything was dim and hazy, and she realised that the sun had fallen almost completely below the suburban rooftops around her. Again, she had worked through the whole afternoon without even knowing what she was doing. She looked before her and saw she had dug a pit directly behind the back wall of her house, a metre wide and just as deep. At the bottom of this hole, bricks the colour of dried blood took over from the cream ranks and grey foundations above... and a few inches above the earthen floor of this new hole, she could see a strip of darker wood set into a frame carved with more of those indecipherable emblems.

It seemed the house before hers had a back door, after all—and a basement that had been missed in the hasty demolition.

Delia fumbled out her phone, took a couple of quick photos with trembling hands. The images were underlit, blurred, nonsensical. She tried to send one to Gustavo and was told that her attempt had failed. Confused, feeling barely at all like herself—or scarcely returned to her own mind after a long spell of opaque anonymity—Delia stumbled away and sought refuge inside. She hadn't the patience to run a bath, so she stood in the steaming shower and wondered if she was losing her mind. It wouldn't be the first time, if her colleagues from her last job were to be believed, or even her high school classmates. Poor old Psycho Delia, off into the fog again.

No! That door was real, though what it portended was unclear. She needed answers, but she knew better than to open that catacomb by night. Besides, she was exhausted and sleep called to soothe her spinning mind, though she'd need some food first if she intended to do anything at all tomorrow. She hung her heavy head and watched as thick ribbons of lobelia-blue swirled around her feet and disappeared into the drain, carried away by unseen pipes... and alongside them, the hidden basement. How had no-one realised the old lady's home contained a lower level when they'd had to demolish the whole building and dig all around it? Had this house been thrown up fast and careless as its garden, a mask swiftly affixed to horrors with more haste than care?

Delia towelled her hair, found it so fair afterward she half-expected to see another face in the mirror. She must redo it again, but not tonight. She barely managed to devour an apple and some cheese before her aching carcass insisted on being dragged back to bed.

> *Are you okay, D? What's going on over there, sweetheart? x*

> *The back door is waiting, lover. Come see me sometime…*

No dreams tonight, just a smothering darkness devoid of light and sound, as though she had been shut away in a chest to keep her from witnessing appalling things. Delia could barely move when she woke, her limbs dead and corpse-heavy. But there was so little work remaining now; she could afford to lie in for a while.

> *Okaaay… you can tell me if things are getting too much again, sugar. Hang in there. I'll be with you before you know it. x*

Delia felt weak as an old lady when she rose, shuffling about the house with the weight of decades hung on her. Her memory might have been going as well, for without recalling it she was dressed and in the open air, the shovel almost slipping from palsied, weeping fingers. But she had the grit of an old woman, too, and barely any time seemed to pass before the pit was two metres deeper and the basement door stood fully revealed. A set of stone steps led down to it, though she'd only uncovered the last four in her eagerness to clear the way.

Time to see. Time to *know*.

Delia threw the shovel aside and slipped down into the pit, the sunhat falling from her unravelling hair. She was glad of the afternoon sky behind her, ensuring she wouldn't be entering the basement blinded by night—a horror-movie move, suited to a Coffineyes soundtrack. She almost raised her hand to knock, then laughed in a voice that was not quite hers and turned the dirty handle. The door opened inward with ease, as though it had been kept oiled all these years.

A slice of sunlight bled inside, and before it weakened to nothing it revealed a decrepit space that looked too familiar for words. This was no fruit cellar, no storage space, but—why?—a kitchen. The splintery wooden table was bare of all but an empty brass bowl, the counter laid with a banquet of furry dust. She stepped in slowly and peered through the murk, her feet gritting on feculent linoleum. Cobwebs danced to the rhythm of her breath. A double-lobed eye stared back at her from the bottom of the bowl. Across the room, a woman swayed and danced, mocking her.

No—nothing but an old dress, swinging slowly on a rusty hanger. She wandered toward it, admiring its glamorous cut even as its unspoken licentiousness repelled her, and beyond the table, just before the light faded to leave only the dress dancing in the dark, she found a strange stain spread upon the parched floor. It might have been oil, for it was black as could be, and it was doubled by a matching taint on the dim ceiling above.

Perhaps something had spoiled and seeped down through the floor of the old house to find a new home here. She knew she shouldn't touch it, refused to, but then her weak legs gave way and she collapsed onto her knees, falling forward, catching herself on her palms as they sank into the stain. The blackness was warm, more so than should have been possible, and if anything, it was—welcoming.

The abyssal nothing of her last dream blossomed, swallowed her senses. Time melted into toxic slurry and she let go the hurts that had plagued her for so long, the whispers of her colleagues, the sneers of her schoolmates. Such feeble fetters were fucking meaningless. She had only to care about one thing, and that was herself. *Her* needs. *Her* pleasures.

And now—

A knocking at the kitchen door.

A grin spread like oil across her mouth. She bridged her split lips with a cautionary finger as something insignificant slipped away into deeper shadows, and then she danced to the door, her best dress swishing around her thighs in a sultry flourish as she opened up to receive her handsome visitor.

She pulled her gentleman caller inside, slamming the door shut with a hungry-hyena laugh, and her smile cut crimson through the dark.

Matthew R. Davis is a Shirley Jackson Award-nominated author and musician from Adelaide, South Australia, with over one hundred short stories and seven books published to date. His latest books are the horror collection SONGS OF SHADOW, WORDS OF WOE *(JournalStone, 2025) and the non-fiction volume* THE CURE ON TRACK: EVERY ALBUM, EVERY SONG *(Sonicbond Publishing, 2025), with an indie film novelisation, a novella, and a novel due for release in 2026. He lives in the suburb of Morphett Vale with the award-winning artist Meg Wright (*Red Wallflower*) and her cats Juniper and Lexi, where Meg's work in the garden and what she found inspired this tale. Find out more at matthewrdavisfiction.wordpress.com.*

MAMMON ESTATES

BY ROSS KILLEY

MAMMON ESTATES

BY ROSS KILLEY

Nicholas staked the FREE sign in his front yard and looked at the pile of assorted junk near the curb. Satisfied, he wiped sweat out of his eyes and went inside to get a cold glass of water. While stretching his back over the sink, Nicholas looked out the back window and saw Christine raking up some of the leftover leaves from Fall. Houdini was out there with her, wagging his tail and rolling around on his back, making a mess of her work.

The sputtering cough of an engine sounded in the driveway.

Nicholas peered out a front window and saw an old blue Chevy. The truck had to have been twenty years past its prime and the same could be said about its driver. The old man got out of his truck in grease covered overalls and walked over to examine the pile of junk. Nicholas had hauled out many items from the home's previous owners that were either damaged or undesirable. The man looked at a skimpy lamp and couch with torn upholstery, then moved on to a dresser missing half its drawers. His gaze fixed on an old washing machine lid.

By the time Nicholas got outside to help, the man had just dropped the scrap metal into the bed of his truck. "Hey, need a hand with anything?"

He looked at Nicholas.

"I guess you got it covered," Nicholas said and reached out his hand in greeting. "My name is Nicholas. My wife and I moved here in January. I'm guessing you live in the neighborhood?"

The older man ignored his friendly gesture and looked at him as if sizing him up. After a few awkward seconds of silence, Nicholas put his hand down. The man had grease marks all over his skin and the unusually hot spring day made it run down his face as if from his pores. The man got back into his truck and shut the door. The engine revived itself and the truck slowly backed out of the driveway. Nicholas watched the Chevy get smaller and smaller, and eventually turn down another street.

If the man did live in the neighborhood, at least he wasn't close. Nicholas and Christine had just moved to Mammon Estates in January and had only met their direct neighbor, George Herman. He was a bachelor that Nicholas had quickly considered a friend. He was glad he lived next to George and not the greasy man.

Nicholas turned, but heard another vehicle stop on the street. Looking back, he saw the window roll down on a police cruiser and a friendly face peered out.

"Hey, is that a bookshelf?" the officer smiled.

"Yeah, you want it?"

"Oh man, my kid loves to read. He'll love this!" Officer Friendly put the cruiser in park and got out. Nicholas grabbed the bookshelf and carried it to the trunk, where the officer stood propping it open. "You think it will fit?"

Nicholas strained to answer as he did all the lifting. "Well, you might have to leave the trunk open a bit. You have any bungee cords?"

"No, but that's okay. I don't live too far from here." His smile never faltered as he watched Nicholas put the shelf in the trunk; he didn't once offer to help. The bookshelf stuck out of the trunk and Officer Friendly carefully lay the lid down over it. "I'll just take it slow from here. Hey, thanks again!" Officer Friendly took Nicholas' hand, shook it almost violently, and got back into the car.

The cruiser was already pulling away when Nicholas realized he hadn't gotten the officer's name.

As the day went on, more and more people came to take the junk that sat in the yard. Nicholas guessed most of them lived in Mammon Estates. Either way, Christine was happy the items were no longer of their concern and that made him happy too.

The hot afternoon faded into cool evening and Nicholas pulled the FREE sign out of the ground, but as he did, he thought he could smell a garbage truck coming. However, it was a lone, disheveled man walking down the sidewalk that he smelt. His clothes were more akin to dirty rags, and he wore a torn cap on his head from which long, dirty strands of grey hair fell. As the homeless looking man got closer, he eyed the sign in Nicholas' hands.

"It's all yours, if you want it," said Nicholas. He held it out and the man took it with arms so frail Nicholas thought they'd break. He left the man to it and started back up the drive until he heard shuffling feet. The man was right behind him, following him up to his house. "Um, did you have a question?"

The man merely looked at him, his face expressionless, totally content. Before Nicholas could say anything else, the man spoke, "You said it was all mine?"

"Excuse me?"

"You said it was all mine, if I wanted it…" The man's words trailed off as he arched his head to the side and looked past Nicholas. "Do you have any more?"

"No, that was the only one. Sorry."

The man's smell festered in the air as he continued to look past Nicholas. His eyes rolled around in his sunken sockets, continuously scanning the house and yard before they stopped and fixated on something. Christine came around the side of the house to place a glass ornament in the front garden and Nicholas realized what the man was staring at. To say it made him uncomfortable that this man staring at his wife in a stupefied gaze of desire, was an understatement.

"Like I said, that's all I have. Sorry." Nicholas could have been rude, but the man hadn't said anything, and he didn't want to create a scene in front of his wife. Luckily, the man's gaze drifted back to Nicholas and a moment later, he was walking back down the sidewalk with his prize.

Nicholas made sure to watch the man until he was completely out of sight. It took a few minutes, but eventually the man turned the same bend the cop had turned down earlier, and Nicholas couldn't be sure, but thought he saw him turn and look back. Eventually, he walked out of sight and Nicholas relaxed.

Nicholas woke up to Christine shaking his shoulder. He'd fallen asleep early and was having nice dreams about raising children in their new home, but now Christine stood over him looking awfully worried. Their Bull

Terrier sat next to her, wagging his tail. He asked her what was wrong, and she told him she'd seen someone in the backyard.

"Are they still there?"

"I don't know. Come look."

At the back door, Nicholas slowly peered around the corner so if someone were out there, they wouldn't see him. Christine stood behind him with Houdini. He could see the deck and the table set that sat upon it. A tree loomed over a quarter of the yard and the fence could be seen a few feet beyond that, but the darkness swallowed it up as if the barrier suddenly ended.

"I'm going to turn the lights on." He flipped the switch and light flooded the area. Now they could see half the backyard and a little beyond the fence.

Christine pointed to the right, "There. On the other side of the fence."

"I'm going to step out and have a look."

"Take Houdini with you."

Nicholas stepped out into the cool night with Houdini. Christine stood in the open doorway, looking in all directions. Nicholas stepped up to the fence and looked to the side of the house and then the neighbor's backyard. He couldn't make out any movement or person-like shapes. "I don't see anything Honey."

"I could've sworn I saw someone. Maybe I'm just too tired and I'm seeing things." She didn't seem too frightened or worried anymore. She went back into the house, Houdini and Nicholas right behind her. Before stepping in, however, Nicholas felt a gentle breeze, and with it came a smell of rotten garbage.

He double-checked all the doors and windows to make sure they were locked before going to bed.

A week went by, and life couldn't have been better. There had been no signs of anyone snooping around the yard and they wrote the incident off. Nicholas blamed the garbage smell on the neighbor's trashcan. Just a coincidence that the draft had brought the smell. No worries.

The weather was magnificent, and the couple decided to walk Houdini around the neighborhood. It was noon and they'd worked up a decent sweat walking half the neighborhood. Houdini was panting and the couple stopped to pour some water in a small bowl. Houdini lapped up the water and Nicholas looked at the dog jealously.

Christine noticed and said, "Don't worry, he'll share."

Nicholas laughed. "Yeah, I suppose we should have brought some for ourselves." They continued walking and within minutes they spotted a little girl running a lemonade stand in front of a house all by herself. "Look at that," said Nicholas with a gratifying smile. "Just what we need."

The couple approached the stand and as they got closer, they noticed what must have been the girl's father, slowly rocking back and forth in a rocking chair on the porch.

By the looks of it, the stand had been hastily nailed together and painted yellow all over. The front read LEMONADE 50 ENT in bright pink paint. The little girl, who wore her best Sunday dress, sat in a chair and was drawing in a coloring book. She looked up and smiled when they approached.

"Hi there, can we buy some lemonade?"

Her smile widened, exposing a missing front tooth. "You want two cups?"

"Yes please," answered Christine. The girl poured the lemonade into plastic cups. Nicholas dug out a dollar bill from his wallet and handed it to the girl.

The girl turned the dollar over in her hand as if she were confused at what it was and then looked back at her father, then back up at the couple. "Do you have any more?"

Nicholas chuckled. "Well, your sign says fifty cents for a cup, and I gave you a dollar." He looked towards the porch where the father had stopped rocking and watched them.

Christine elbowed Nicholas in the side. "Honey, just give her another dollar."

The last thing he wanted to do was to argue a point to the girl in front of her father, so Nicholas retrieved another dollar and handed it to the girl. She examined it just like the first, and then smiled at them, "Thank you."

"You're welcome," Christine said as they walked away with their cups. Nicholas turned to look back at the house; the father went back to rocking in his chair and the girl gave Nicholas that missing-tooth smile.

A few days later Christine noticed a glass ornament had disappeared from the garden. She told Nicholas as soon as he had come home from work, and they talked about it over lasagna.

"Which one?" Nicholas asked.

"The one that looked like a sunflower."

He remembered it. The ornament was blown from glass of many colors, and when the light hit just right, it looked dazzling.

"Who would have taken it?"

Christine looked defeated, "Kids maybe?"

Nicholas didn't have an answer for her. Why would someone steal an ornament that you could buy at any lawn store? He promised to buy her a new one.

The sun had set and the couple were loading the dirty dishes into the washer when they heard a small crash outside.

"What was that?" Christine sounded wary.

"Sounded like the trash bin falling over."

Christine continued loading the dishwasher while Nicholas walked back into the dining room and looked out the window. He was right. The trash bin had caused the noise, but it hadn't fallen, it was pushed.

Three people stood at the end of the driveway, rummaging through the garbage that had spilled onto the street. It was dark out and Nicholas couldn't tell who it was, but he had an idea of who it might be. Nicholas went into the kitchen and grabbed a flashlight from a cupboard.

"What was it?" Christine asked.

"I think some homeless people are going through our garbage." Christine said something, but in his haste, he didn't hear what. He was out the front door and across the lawn before he knew it and turned the light on the curb.

He expected to see the homeless man and maybe some of his buddies going through the trash, but the people Nicholas saw didn't look homeless at all. One was a woman who looked to be in her late thirties, another was a man of the same age and wearing a ball cap, and the last person was a kid who could have been as young as sixteen. They looked like a family.

"What are you guys doing?" His voice was curious yet stern; Nicholas wanted to know why they were going through his trash. His question went unanswered for as soon as the words left his mouth, the three scavengers bolted in different directions. "Wait!"

Nicholas thought about running after them, but which one? What would he do if he caught them? After all, they only knocked over his trash. That wasn't exactly a criminal offense. Before he could decide, the trio disappeared into the night.

Dumbfounded, Nicholas cleaned up the trash. When he went back inside, Christine stood in the living room looking worried. "What happened? I saw people running off." He told her all of what happened. "Should we call the police?"

"They aren't going to do anything. Once garbage hits the curb its public property. Plus, I didn't get a great look at them and have no idea where they ran off to. The police will see it as a waste of time."

"Well, we should do something. I mean, I saw someone in the backyard, then someone stole an ornament right out of the yard and now we have people going through our trash."

"You *thought* you saw someone in the back yard." Nicholas knew she was becoming agitated. "But if it makes you feel better, I'll buy a bat or something."

"A bat?"

"Yeah, a baseball bat."

Christine folded her arms and looked unimpressed. "How about a gun?"

"A gun?" Nicholas sounded almost shocked. "You want me to buy a gun because a lawn ornament went missing and a few people went through our trash?"

"I don't care for guns either Nick, but it would make me feel a whole lot better knowing we could defend ourselves if we had to." With that, she walked back into the kitchen.

Nicholas sighed, then checked all the locks on the doors and windows.

They were walking Houdini on his leash again. It was warm out, but there was a bit of overcast above their heads. They found themselves on the same street as they had a few days ago where the girl had the lemonade stand and sure enough, she was there again.

"She's back at it," said Christine. "Bet she won't get many customers today." Nicholas nodded in agreement, and they walked on the other side of the street, but that didn't stop the girl from looking up to smile. There was no sign of the father on the porch.

Stopping only to let Houdini pee on a few hydrants and stop signs, they turned onto a street in the neighborhood they hadn't been down before and decided to follow where it went. An elderly woman watered her flowers close by. Houdini led them past the woman's house, but Christine grabbed Nicholas' arm.

"Did you see that?" she asked.

"What?"

"Did you see what was in her yard?" Nicholas hadn't been paying attention and shook his head. "It was my ornament. The one that was stolen."

"The same one?" He looked back at the yard.

"Don't stare," she hissed.

He didn't and she waited for him to say something. "What? You think that old lady stole it from our yard?"

Christine stared hard. "It's the same one, Nick."

"You can't possibly know that. We weren't that close to it, and you know it's possible she may own the same one."

Christine shook her head and continued walking with Houdini.

Nicholas stayed put and looked back at the house; the woman had gone inside. He scanned the yard and a hint of ruby glass stuck out from a bush.

An SUV drove up between Nicholas and the house, blocking his view. He saw the driver was a man wearing a ball cap. For a split second, the driver turned his head and looked at Nicholas, then turned his eyes back to the road as he drove past Christine and Houdini. The SUV turned down a street and was gone. Nicholas thought it looked an awful lot like the man who'd gone through his trash.

"Are you coming or what?" Christine asked. "I think it might rain."

An afternoon shower hit shortly after they made it home. Christine hadn't brought up the lawn ornament again and Nicholas didn't know what she wanted him to do about it. Did she expect him to march over there and take an old lady's lawn ornament out of her yard? Nicholas was not about to make a fool of himself by doing that. He'd rather just buy her a new one.

George Herman called shortly after the rain stopped.

Nicholas spoke into the phone. "Hey George, what's up?"

"Hey buddy, how's it goin'?" His voice carried a certain upbeat energy to it that was infectious.

"Not a whole lot. Christine and I walked Houdini earlier and made it home just before the rain started."

"Yeah, it really came down there for a little bit. You got anything going on at the moment?"

"No, why?"

"Well, I'm trying out a new recipe and I forgot to buy eggs. Would you have a couple to spare?"

"I think we got some. Meet you outside in a few minutes?"

"Sure thing buddy!"

Nicholas found three eggs in the fridge and walked them next door. George was standing in his side yard wearing workout shorts and a tank top that was too small for his portly frame. He was looking up at the sky. "Looks like it might start up again."

"Beats snow, right?" Nicholas handed over the eggs. "Having some guests over or something?"

His gaze left the sky. "I might. Not sure yet. But I found this awesome new recipe for cookies, and I just really needed these eggs. I hate running to the store for one thing and at this time of day it's probably a zoo."

"Yeah, you're probably right," Nicholas chuckled. "Have you noticed anything weird going on lately? Around the neighborhood?"

He gave Nicholas a quizzical look. "What do you mean?"

Nicholas told him about all the peculiar events he and Christine had experienced as of late.

George shook his head, "Can't say that I've noticed anything. I've seen people go through trash before. It's like a weird hobby for some. I'd have to imagine you're going to find some odd balls in any neighborhood. Christine really thinks that lady stole her lawn ornament?"

"Yeah."

"Sheesh. I don't know man. As far as the peeping toms in your yard, you should invest in some automatic security lights. That'll scare them away."

Nicholas nodded. "I might try that. Well, I'll let you get back to cooking. But let me know if you see anything weird, okay?"

"Yeah, no problem buddy." George looked down at the small cartoon of eggs in his hands for the first time and noticed there were only three eggs. Nicholas had already turned around when George asked, "Hey, do you have any more?"

It rained throughout the night, leaving a fine layer of sparkling morning dew on everyone's lawns. Houdini, needing to be let out, woke Nicholas. Christine didn't wake to his whines, so Nicholas left her sleeping. He let Houdini out and started the coffee machine. Once his mug filled, he stepped outside with it. Houdini was walking circles around the tree, probably sniffing out a squirrel. Nicholas smiled and brought the mug to his lips, but stopped there.

There were impressions in the grass.

He walked over to one and looked down. It was a shoe impression. A whole line of them came from the corner of the yard near the fence. Nicholas stared long and hard at them. They were too big to be from Christine and he hadn't stepped foot in the backyard at all yesterday. He walked over to the fence and saw that they kept going on the other side.

Nicholas looked behind him and followed the impressions back through the yard and up to the bedroom window.

"What the hell..."

Nicholas couldn't see much through the curtain, but when he strained his eyes, he could just make out the sleeping form of Christine. He backed up a few steps and then looked around, as if the person who had entered their yard was still around. He looked back down. The shoe prints were very noticeable in the wet mulch.

Nicholas thought about whether to tell Christine about what he'd found. After a minute, he used his foot to screw up the mulch. He might tell her, but not right away. He didn't want to send her into a panic. Instead, Nicholas decided he would go shopping.

Nicholas left right after Christine went to work. Security lights were purchased at the hardware store and once home it took two hours to install one in the front yard and one in the back. He thought it would take longer, but they made them so any moron could install them nowadays. Both were tested and he was happy with the results. The lights would turn on as soon as someone stepped within thirty feet. Once done, he went into the kitchen where another purchase sat on the table.

He reached into the bag and brought out a small case, flipped the latches on it, and opened the lid to reveal the pistol.

The nine-millimeter was small in his hands. He hadn't shot many guns in his life, but Nicholas trusted the man working at the sporting goods store and handed over the four hundred dollars. After a quick background check, he was allowed to walk out of the store with the gun.

Nicholas loaded the magazine, but didn't put it in the pistol. Instead, he walked into the bedroom and put both items next to each other in his nightstand. Hopefully, he'd never use it.

It just got dark by the time Christine came home from work. She had a sack of takeout in her arms. They ate at the dining room table and talked about her day. "It was slow for me," she said. "What did you do today?"

"I bought some security lights and installed them in the front and back."

"Really?" She looked somewhat surprised. "I didn't see them come on when I came home."

"I have them set to only come on when it gets dark out. Figured it would deter any old ladies from coming into our yard." He was glad to see that Christine found the comment funny.

They talked, ate, and as time went by, Nicholas realized he forgot to tell her about the gun. He decided to hold off on telling her for now. They were having a good time and he wanted to enjoy it.

They let Houdini outside and began cleaning off the table when Christine said, "Hey, the light came on." Nicholas stopped what he was doing and could see the bright light through the living room curtains. "You hear that?"

Nicholas ran to the window and pushed the curtain aside. In the cone of light, he could make out a hunched figure in the driveway, between their cars.

"Someone's out there." He ran to the bedroom, grabbed the pistol and slid the magazine in before heading to the front door.

"Where did that come from?" Christine asked, concerned. "And what are you going to do with it?"

"From the store. Come stand by the door and be ready to lock it if anything happens." Christine seemed confused but did as she was told. Without warning, Nicholas went out the door.

Nicholas approached the cars. The gun in his hand made him feel better, even if he held it behind his back. He didn't want anyone to see him walking with a gun in plain sight if he could help it. An odd sound came from between the cars where the person bent over a tire. Coming around the car, he saw a man using a lug wrench to take off the rim.

"What the hell is going on?" Nicholas shouted. The man looked up. Nicholas recognized him as the older man with the blue Chevy who had taken the washing machine lid. He was again grimy and covered in grease. The man spun the lug wrench free, pocketing the nut that came with it. Nicholas pulled the gun out from behind him and pointed it at the man. "Put the wrench down and tell me what you're doing."

The man stood up, but didn't put the wrench down. He didn't seem afraid of the weapon. Before Nicholas could do or say anything, he saw more people out of the corner of his eye. Details were lost in the gloom of the security light, but it looked to be a handful of people, all walking towards his yard from the sidewalk. Then another group of people came from the left. The man with the wrench stood rock still.

A bad feeling formed in the pit of his stomach and Nicholas ran to the front door and pushed his way inside, almost knocking down Christine. He threw the door shut and bolted it.

"I called the cops," she said, panicking. "What's going on?"

"Quiet!" He heard footsteps on the porch and looked through the peephole. A handful of people stood around on the porch, looking around as if they'd never seen a porch before. One by one, Nicholas started to recognize them as people that lived in the neighborhood. But what were they doing at his house? A figure Nicholas recognized immediately walked up to the porch, pushed his way through the small crowd, and stood right in front of the door.

Nicholas could smell him through the door.

The homeless man looked right at the peephole and grinned. Something was hefted up to the hole. It took Nicholas a second to register what it was. It was the FREE sign he'd given to the man.

"What the fuck," Nicholas whispered.

The sign lowered out of view, and the homeless man got so close to the peephole that Nicholas could only see the man's tongue as it rolled around his few rotten teeth. "Do you have any more?" His voice mocked. "You said it was all mine if I wanted it!" The man began laughing.

Nicholas reared from the door.

"I'm scared, Nick." Christine was almost in tears, and he didn't know what to say to her.

It began to sound like a circus outside as they heard more and more voices surrounding their house. Both went to the window and peaked through the curtains. What they saw just didn't make sense. The people of Mammon Estates were everywhere. Their very neighbors! Nicholas saw the man in overalls back to work on his tires while others began to break into the cars, smashing at the handles and windows with various items and tools. The old lady that'd stolen the glass ornament bent over Christine's garden and began plucking whole flowers right out of the ground and holding them up victoriously.

Christine was crying. "Why are they doing this?"

"I don't know why they're doing it, but if they try to get in, they'll be sorry."

Just then, the power in the house went out and they heard barking from the backyard.

"Oh my God, Houdini!" Christine ran to the back door. Nicholas grabbed her before she opened the door to run out. "Let me go!"

"Look!" Nicholas pointed out the window. It was dark out now that the lights had lost power, but that didn't stop them from seeing dark forms climbing over the fence line. There were at least fifteen people climbing into their back yard, probably more.

Three of them stood out as the family that had raided his garbage. The teenage boy was first over the fence and before his foot touched the ground, Houdini ran up and bit his calf. The boy let out a wail and fell to the ground as Houdini began tearing and tugging. The mother hopped over the fence and tried to pull Houdini off her boy. She came away with the dog in her hands, while her son wiggled on the ground holding his torn leg. Houdini growled and reeled back and forth in her arms, trying to bite her. The father, wearing the same ball cap as he did in the SUV, stepped up from the other side of the fence and clubbed Houdini over the head with a brick. The dog went limp, and the mother handed him over to the father who took him and began to walk away with him. Nicholas had no way of knowing if Houdini was alive or not.

Christine sagged to the floor and began to weep. Nicholas wanted to hold her and tell her everything would be all right, but he couldn't believe half the things he was seeing. He tucked the pistol in his waistband and managed to pick Christine up off the floor and drag her to the living room where he sat her down.

Red and blue lights began to flash through the curtains and all the noise came to a halt.

After a minute, Nicholas got up and went to look out the peephole. He saw a cop standing with his back to the door. Nicolas looked at his wife. "The cops are here. Everything is going to be okay. We're going to get Houdini back." She looked at him with tearful eyes but didn't say anything. Nicholas unbolted the door and swung it open.

Officer Friendly turned and smiled at Nicholas. "Howdy neighbor. The station got a call from here and I figured since I live on the other side of the neighborhood that I'd come check it out. What seems to be the problem?"

Nicholas was at a loss for words. Hadn't he seen all the people that were outside? Where'd they go? What about all the damage to the cars and yard?

"Hey, you know my kid loved that bookshelf," Officer Friendly said, still smiling. "You wouldn't happen to have any more would you?"

Nicholas reached behind his back for the pistol, but Officer Friendly had his out first. A loud ringing filled Nicholas' ears and he felt a white-hot heat in his gut. He fell back into the house.

"Nicholas!" Christine screamed and crawled up to him, covering his leaking wound with her hands. The couple watched in horror as the neighbors who'd hid in the yard filed past Officer Friendly and into the house. They started going through everything the couple owned, taking whatever they wanted.

Christine reached for the gun that had fallen onto the ground, but Officer Friendly stomped on her hand, then took the gun for himself. "Sorry Miss. You two seem like nice folks, but it's Offering Season and there ain't nothing that can be done about that."

More and more people filled the house until all of the neighborhood had to be in attendance. Within minutes, half the stuff in the house had been pillaged. They were leaving almost nothing behind and the stuff they did ended up on the floor broken and smashed.

Despite the pain in his gut, Nicholas was conscious of it all, even when the homeless man walked through the door and grabbed up Christine with those frail arms. She struggled, kicking and screaming. The man's skeletal form possessed more strength than it ought to, and he dragged Christine out the front door. Nicholas heard her cries trail off in the night.

George Herman walked in and grabbed the flat screen TV off its stand. "Sorry buddy. I hate to do this to a nice guy like you, but I've got guests coming over later and this would look really nice on my wall, and then there's the Offering..." He looked down at Nicholas with sorrow in his eyes. "I hope we can still be friends." Then he was out of the house.

Nicholas tried to yell, scream, anything to halt the madness, but the pain from the gunshot was too great. A small figure came prancing through the front door. It was the girl from the lemonade stand. She bent over Nicholas and gave him that missing tooth grin. With her hands, she pried open his mouth. He could feel her tiny fingers snag onto his front left tooth and pull. The pain was excruciating. Nerves burst and the tooth loosened up, then came free. She held up her prize with bloody hands and waved it at her father who was standing on the porch, an approving smile on his face. "Thanks!" she said and ran back out the door.

Nicholas lay bleeding out on the floor. Officer Friendly stood turning the pistol over in his hands, happy with his find. An older man with a cane almost stumbled as he came into the house. He began waving the cane back and forth and it landed on Nicholas' leg. A smile came to the man's lips. He dropped the cane to the ground and bent over, running his hands over Nicholas' face. They found his eyes. "Ahhh, what have we here?"

The man's fingers felt like talons and Nicholas closed his eyes before they sank in. He finally screamed.

The car rolled into the neighborhood and passed the entrance sign.

"Mammon Estates. What does that even mean?" the teen asked her parents from the back seat.

"I don't know sweetie," her mother said. "But your father and I got a great deal on this house."

The daughter took out her phone and ran a search on Mammon. Her face scrunched in confusion when she saw the result.

Her phone read:

In the New Testament, it's commonly thought to mean money, material and wealth. In the Middle Ages it was often personified as a deity and sometimes known as one of the Seven Princes of Hell.

His mom would tell you his father got him hooked on horror movies at too young an age. Although a 90's kid, Ross Killey has had a steady diet of everything from* Abbott and Costello Meet Frankenstein *to* Dawn of the Dead. *He works security full time and reads and writes when his daughter is taking naps. Ross lives in central Indiana with his family and is the author of* Full Moon Highway, Stuck to a Monster *and* Nightmare Jungle.

COMMUNITY COVENANT

AN EPISTOLARY FABLE

BY S E HOWARD

COMMUNITY COVENANT

AN EPISTOLARY FABLE BY S.E. HOWARD

July 12, 20XX

Dear ANDREW J. & SIMONE E. COLSON:

Please be advised that your property located at 4121 LARK-SPUR LANE is in violation of the Garden SpringsTM Community Covenants, Conditions, and Restrictions (CCCR) Agreement.

You have recently added updates to your landscaping that are not included in our list of approved plants, shrubs, and trees. For your reference, we have enclosed copies of the approved and prohibited plant lists and images of the offending vegetation. Please remove these items within 30 days of this notification. Failure to comply will result in corrective action being taken.

Your prompt attention to this matter is appreciated. Should you have any questions or concerns, please direct any written correspondence to the address listed below.

Sincerely,

Your Neighbors on the Board of the Homeowners Association (HOA)

The Planned Community of Garden Springs™

July 15, 20XX

Dear Members of the HOA Board:

I am in receipt of your letter from July 12 citing landscaping violations in our yard. I think a mistake has been made, and wanted to take this opportunity to clarify.

My wife Simone is a third grade teacher at Buckley Elementary School. Before the end of the school year, Simone's mother passed away unexpectedly, causing her to miss more than a week of classes in order to arrange and attend the funeral. She explained her absence to her students ahead of time, and shared with them that sunflowers had always been her mother's favorite, and reminded Simone of happy times with her family. The children in her class put together a sunflower-themed gift basket, which they gave to her upon her return from bereavement leave.

This gift contained a packet of seeds for a variety of sunflowers called "Del Sol." Simone planted these seeds in the backyard along the fence line of our property, and some have recently started to bloom. Del Sol sunflowers don't grow as large as other varieties. None of ours are taller than our fence. Again, I should emphasize that Simone planted these in the back yard not the front, and they are not immediately visible from the street. Furthermore, we checked the HOA list before planting, and didn't see them as being prohibited.

These were a thoughtful gift from Simone's students that provided her with comfort during an otherwise very difficult time. Given this, and the points mentioned above, I do not feel we are in violation of the CCCR Agreement.

Respectfully,
Drew Colson

July 19, 20XX

Dear ANDREW J. & SIMONE E. COLSON:

This is your SECOND NOTICE OF VIOLATION.

Your property located at 4121 LARKSPUR LANE is in violation of the Garden SpringsTM Community Covenants, Conditions, and Restrictions (CCCR) Agreement.

You have recently added updates to your landscaping that are not included in our list of approved plants, shrubs, and trees. These guidelines are in place to ensure consistency in our overall neighborhood aesthetic. Any deviation could negatively impact property values, as well as pose safety issues or pest control concerns.

Please be advised you now have 24 DAYS to remove these items. Failure to comply will result in corrective action being taken.

Sincerely,

Your Neighbors on the Board of the Homeowners Association (HOA)

The Planned Community of Garden Springs™

July 20, 20XX

Dear HOA Board:

I received a second notice of violation from you today, again regarding sunflowers my wife planted in our backyard that are NOT in violation of the CCCR Agreement. We have reviewed the list of prohibited plants line by line and SUNFLOWERS AREN'T INCLUDED.

Additionally, these flowers are in the backyard, which is enclosed by a fence, meaning the plants aren't visible to anyone either driving or walking past our house. Therefore, they can't possibly disrupt any "neighborhood aesthetic," much less adversely impact property value. As previously mentioned, none are tall enough to hide prospective burglars from view, so they don't pose a safety issue. And as far as possible pests, I have yet to notice any locust swarms or rodent hordes in our flower bed, which indicates to me the sunflowers pose no significant risk for that, either.

I don't know who is taking the photographs you keep sending to us, but clearly they were in our backyard, which means they were TRESPASSING on our private property. I think that would be a bigger concern to the HOA.

Regards,

Andrew Colson

From a thread posted to the Garden Springs TM Community message board:

Andrew Colson – Larkspur Lane ● July 20 ● 6:15 p.m.
Someone keeps coming onto my property to take pictures in my back yard. Hoping someone across the street has doorbell cam footage that might help me figure out who it is!

> **Reply from Braden Ramsey – Larkspur Lane ● July 20 ● 6:20 p.m.**
> Sorry man. No such luck.

> **Reply from Jeremy Leonard – Larkspur Lane ● July 20 ● 6:35 p.m.**
> We have a Ring camera, but think we're too far down the block. You're at 4121, right?

> **Reply from Olivia Goldman – Bradford Avenue ● July 20 ● 8:07 p.m.**
> That's really scary! You should let the HOA know.

>> **Reply from Andrew Colson – Larkspur Lane ● July 20 ● 8:15 p.m.**
>> Someone on the HOA is doing it.

> **Reply from Olivia Goldman – Bradford Avenue ● July 20 ● 8:22 p.m.**
> What??? How do you know?

>> **Reply from Andrew Colson – Larkspur Lane ● July 20 ● 8:26 p.m.**
>> Because the HOA keeps sending me the pictures along with notices of violation. My wife planted sunflowers and they say they're not allowed.

>>> **Reply from Olivia Goldman – Bradford Avenue ● July 20 ● 8:27 p.m.**
>>> There's a list of approved and prohibited plants. You should have checked first.

>>> **Reply from Andrew Colson – Larkspur Lane ● July 20 ● 8:34 p.m.**
>>> We DID check. No mention of sunflowers!

Reply from Olivia Goldman – Bradford Avenue ● July 20 ● 9:07 p.m.
Well that's just strange then.

Reply from Andrew Colson – Larkspur Lane ● July 20 ● 10:12 p.m.
I know right??

Reply from Michael Duncan – Rose Trellis Way ● July 21 ● 8:01 a.m.
No offense, but if the HOA's sending you violation notices, you ought to just get rid of the sunflowers.

Reply from Alejandro Martinez – Lilac Bloom Way ● July 21 ● 12:30 p.m.
Yeah don't they only give you like 30 days? How long's this been going on?

Reply from Andrew Colson – Larkspur Lane ● July 21 ● 2:11 p.m.
Just over a week now. It's bullshit. We haven't done anything wrong.

Reply from Alejandro Martinez – Lilac Bloom Way ● July 21 ● 4:26 p.m.
Yeah but if the HOA says to get rid of them, you should just do it.

Reply from Andrew Colson – Larkspur Lane ● July 21 ● 5:09 p.m.
WE DIDN'T DO ANYTHING WRONG.

Reply from Catherine O'Malley – Bradford Avenue ● July 21 ● 8:17 p.m.
They can fine you. Or put a lien on your home. Foreclose even.

Reply from Andrew Colson – Larkspur Lane ● July 21 ● 8:35 p.m.
Over SUNFLOWERS????

July 22, 20XX

Dear ANDREW J. & SIMONE E. COLSON:

Please be advised that your property located at 4121 LARK-SPUR LANE is in violation of policy 5.1.3A.iii of the Garden Springs™ Community Covenants, Conditions, and Restrictions (CCCR) Agreement prohibiting yard signs.

For your reference, we have enclosed images of the offending item(s). Please remove these immediately upon receipt of this notification. Failure to comply will result in corrective action being taken.

Sincerely,

Your Neighbors on the Board of the Homeowners Association (HOA)

The Planned Community of Garden Springs™

Andrew Colson – Larkspur Lane ● July 22 ● 5:47 p.m.
Does anyone know how to contact members of the HOA? There are no phone numbers or email addresses listed on the website, just a P.O. Box.

> **Reply from Braden Ramsey – Larkspur Lane ● July 22 ● 6:10 p.m.**
> I think you have to write them a letter.

> > **Reply from Andrew Colson – Larkspur Lane ● July 22 ● 8:19 p.m.**
> > I mean who are the members? Where can I find their names so I can try to reach them individually? This thing with the sunflowers is getting out of hand. I need to talk to a real person.

> > > **Reply from Braden Ramsey – Larkspur Lane ● July 22 ● 10:20 p.m.**
> > > Sorry man. Have no idea.

Reply from Andrew Colson – Larkspur Lane ● July 22 ● 11:02 p.m.
It's like they don't even exist. Like they're ghosts.

Reply from Braden Ramsey – Dahlia Trail ● July 23 ● 9:07 p.m.
Or the devil, am I right?

Reply from ● Andrew Colson – Larkspur Lane July 23 ● 11:32 p.m.
LOL exactly

July 23, 20XX

Dear HOA Board:

I put No Trespassing signs on my fence after you repeatedly contacted me about the sunflowers my wife planted being in violation of the CCCR Agreement. With each notice of this so-called "violation," you enclosed pictures of the "offending vegetation" that were clearly obtained while you (or whoever is working for you) TRESPASSED ON MY PROPERTY.

I have explained multiple times that sunflowers are not listed among the prohibited plants in the CCCR, nor are they visible to anyone else in the neighborhood except for me and my wife, because they are in our fenced-in back yard. Despite this, you continue to claim we are somehow in violation, and now you're citing me for signs I posted to keep you from illegally coming onto my property.

This is ridiculous. Stay the hell out of my yard.

Andrew Colson

July 25, 20XX

Dear ANDREW J. & SIMONE E. COLSON:

For clarification purposes, you are not being cited for the use of plants that are included on our list of prohibited vegetation. Rather, the offending items are not listed on our APPROVED plants list. Per policy 5.0.32B.iv of the Garden Springs™ Community Covenants, Conditions, and Restrictions (CCCR) Agreement, any landscaping additions not specifically included on either the approved or prohibited lists are to be submitted in writing for Board consideration. You did not complete the required request and therefore, you are in violation of the CCCR Agreement.

Sincerely,

Your Neighbors on the Board of the Homeowners Association (HOA)

The Planned Community of Garden Springs™

July 25, 20XX

Are you kidding? You're saying even though sunflowers aren't specifically prohibited, they're not exactly allowed, either, and I should have asked for your permission to plant them in MY OWN YARD???

You people are out of your damn minds.

Andrew Colson

August 2, 20XX

Dear ANDREW J. & SIMONE E. COLSON:

This is your THIRD NOTICE OF VIOLATION.

Your property located at 4121 LARKSPUR LANE is in violation of the Garden Springs™ Community Covenants, Conditions, and Restrictions (CCCR) Agreement. You have recently added updates to your landscaping that are not included in our list of approved plants, shrubs, and trees.

Please be advised you now have 10 DAYS to remove the noncompliant elements from your property. Failure to do so will result in corrective action being taken.

Sincerely,

Your Neighbors on the Board of the Homeowners Association (HOA)

The Planned Community of Garden Springs™

August 5, 20XX

Dear Whoever The Hell You Are:

Why is there no public listing of your members? I checked the Garden Springs website, the Better Business Bureau, and the Attorney General's office, but no one seems to have any idea who "you" actually are. Are you one person or a hundred? Are you even a person at all?

I will not remove the signs until you stop trespassing on my property. I will not remove the sunflowers because they are not in violation of the CCCR. I intend to seek legal counsel, so you can expect to hear from my attorney in the immediate future.

Andrew J. Colson

From: hannah.morales@meyermoralesandyoungLLP.com
Subject: Garden Springs Homeowners Association
Date: 10 August 20XX 12:00:42

Dear Mr. Colson,

Thank you very much for contacting the law offices of Meyer, Morales, and Young LLP. While we empathize with your frustration over your present circumstances, we regret that we will be unable to assist with your legal needs.

Unfortunately, because the Garden Springs Community Covenants, Conditions, and Restrictions Agreement complies with state and local statutes, the Homeowners Association is well within their enforcement rights in this matter. When you signed a copy of this CCCR, you entered into a legally binding agreement with the management entity of Garden Springs and as such, you are bound by the terms of that contract.

However, many HOAs are willing to negotiate for reasonable exceptions and accommodations to their bylaws and regulations. We encourage you to continue pursuing meaningful dialogue to see if a mutually beneficial agreement on this matter can be reached.

As an alternative, you could also just dig up the sunflowers.

Sincerely,

Hannah E. Morales, Esq.

Attorney-at-Law

Andrew Colson – Larkspur Lane ● August 11 ● 9:42 p.m.
Do you remember what you said before about the HOA board being the devil?

Reply from Braden Ramsey – Larkspur Lane ● August 11 ● 9:53 p.m.
Ha ha yeah

Reply from Andrew Colson – Larkspur Lane ● August 11 ● 9:57 p.m.
I think you might be on to something. I asked a lawyer if they could help and they told me when we signed the CCCR, we entered into a legally binding agreement with the management entity. That's what they called it: an entity.

Reply from Braden Ramsey – Larkspur Lane ● August 11 ● 10:02 p.m.
Ha ha

Reply from Andrew Colson – Larkspur Lane ● August 11 ● 10:05 p.m.
I'm serious. I think we signed away our souls or something.

Reply from Braden Ramsey – Larkspur Lane ● August 11 ● 10:06 p.m.
Ha ha sounds about right.

August 12, 20XX

Dear ANDREW J. & SIMONE E. COLSON:

This is your FINAL NOTICE OF VIOLATION. Your property located at 4121 LARKSPUR LANE is in violation of the Garden SpringsTM Community Covenants, Conditions, and Restrictions (CCCR) Agreement. Because you have failed to correct these violations within the time-frame allowed, you will now face corrective action.

Sincerely,

Your Neighbors on the Board of the Homeowners Association (HOA)

The Planned Community of Garden SpringsTM

August 12, 20XX

Dear HOA:

GO FUCK YOURSELVES WITH A SUNFLOWER.

Regards,
A. Colson

Wayne Kolowski – Primrose Lane ● August 12 ● 7:22 p.m.
Any idea what's happening on Larkspur Lane??? Was out walking the dog and heard a woman screaming her head off. Couldn't tell which house it was coming from.

Reply from Natasha Gutenberg – Primrose Lane ● August 12 ● 8:10 p.m.
Police have the whole street blocked off now. 💀

Reply from Braden Ramsey – Larkspur Lane ● August 12 ● 8:24 p.m.
No clue what's going on but just saw a couple of Crime Scene Investigation vans go by.

Reply from Jeremy Leonard – Larkspur Lane ● August 12 ● 9:30 p.m.
We live on the other end of the block but can see from our porch. At least a dozen squad cars, two ambulances, and a bunch of CSI.

Reply from Charlie Clifford – Wisteria Avenue ● August 12 ● 9:31 p.m.
They're at 4121 Larkspur Lane. I heard it on my police scanner.

Reply from Natasha Gutenberg – Primrose Lane ● August 12 ● 9:34 p.m.
OMG did they say what happened???

Reply from Charlie Clifford – Wisteria Avenue ● August 12 ● 9:35 p.m.
There's a woman inside the house with her throat slit. And a man who got stabbed more than 70 times. Both DOA.

> **Reply from Natasha Gutenberg – Primrose Lane ● August 12 ● 9:35 p.m.**
> OMG

> **Reply from Charlie Clifford – Wisteria Avenue ● August 12 ● 9:36 p.m.**
> They said it's a real mess. Whoever did it cut out the guy's eyes. His tongue too. "A ritualistic killing," that's what they called it.

> **Reply from Natasha Gutenberg – Primrose Lane ● August 12 ● 9:35 p.m.**
> Like a cult or something? Did they catch who did it? Are we safe???

Reply from Andrea Mendez –Bradford Avenue ● August 12 ● 9:31 p.m.
Isn't that where Drew Colson lives?

> **Reply from Wayne Kolowski – Primrose Lane ● August 12 ● 9:31 p.m.**
> Who?

> > **Reply from Andrea Mendez – Bradford Avenue ● August 12 ● 9:32 p.m.**
> > The guy with the sunflowers

August 15, 20XX

Dear Residents:

As you may or may not be aware, on the evening of August 12, police were called to the residence of our neighbors Andrew and Simone Colson at 4121 Larkspur Lane in response to a domestic disturbance complaint. With rumors of a home invasion or devil worship involvement running rampant, we wanted to reassure that the safety and security of all residents in The Planned Community of Garden SpringsTM is our utmost priority. Therefore, with the permission of law enforcement, we would like to share the preliminary results of their investigation.

There was no sign of forced entry at the scene and no fingerprints or forensic evidence to indicate anyone other than Simone and Andrew Colson were present in the home at the time of their deaths. Police therefore believe that Simone attacked and killed her husband with a kitchen knife before committing suicide.

While we may never know what triggered such horrific violence, investigators have developed a theory. Simone Colson's mother passed away earlier this year, and family describe her as going through "a very difficult time" as a result. As an elementary school teacher, she was home for the summer, and thus away from the support of friends in her workplace. Police believe this sense of isolation, compounded with grief at her mother's death, led her to commit the terrible acts of August 12.

Those of you who knew Andrew and Simone are encouraged to attend their funeral services, and we are enclosing details with this correspondence. Additionally, the HOA Board has had a memorial arrangement of Del Sol sunflowers delivered to the funeral home on behalf of the entire community. "Del Sol" means "of the sun," and we hope these blooms will represent the light and warmth that Andrew and Simone brought to the lives of their friends and neighbors here in Garden Springs TM.

Please join us in keeping Andrew, Simone, and their family in our thoughts and of course, our prayers.

Sincerely,

Your Neighbors on the Board of the Homeowners Association (HOA)

The Planned Community of Garden Springs^{TM}

S.E. Howard lives in Kentucky where she works as a registered nurse, certified in toxicology (a fitting field given her side-hustle writing horror stories). Her short stories have appeared in numerous anthologies, including **PUSH! An Anthology of Childbirth Horror** *presented by Ruth Anna Evans,* **Carnival of Horror** *from Undertaker Books, and the Amber, Sinister, Green Diamond, and Blood Red Editions of* **The Horror Collection** *by KJK Publishing. Her short story "You've Been Saved" was also adapted for the screen in the 2022 GenreBlast film anthology* **Worst Laid Plans.** *Her debut horror novel* **The Vessel** *is available now from Aethon Books/Wicked House, with the follow-up,* **What Lies Unseen,** *coming in March 2026. Find out more at www.sehoward.com.*

NIGHT WHISPERS

BY JASON GARMAN

NIGHT WHISPERS

BY JASON GARMAN

Standing on the edge of the canyon of consciousness, the tethers of compos mentis disengage from reality. Sleep opens like a black flower, petals curling inward until the mind folds in on itself. Light is remembered only as pressure, sound as tremor, identity as a fading echo. In that abyss, everything is true for an instant before it is erased.

He woke with a start, though nothing had stirred him. No alarm, no sound in the house, not even a dream he could put his finger on. Just that sudden, weightless snap into consciousness — like a diver breaking the surface of a lake. Lungs burning, no memory of the plunge.

For a moment, he lay still, staring into the dark ceiling, the quiet pressed close around him.

His wife's slow breathing steadied in the pillow beside him, the dogs curled in their usual sprawl at the foot of the bed. All normal. Perfectly normal.

And yet.

Something in the air hummed, low and sour, like a fluorescent bulb on the edge of dying. He couldn't see it, couldn't hear it, but it was there, vibrating just under the skin. His chest tightened with the feeling that he'd woken from a dream — an important one, urgent even — but it had evaporated the second he opened his eyes. Now all that was left was the aftertaste of meaning, a message unsent.

He swallowed, dry-mouthed, and glanced at the glowing red numbers on the nightstand clock. Too late, too early. One of those times that didn't feel like part of the night but rather a stray pocket of it, a misplaced hour.

He shifted, uneasily, though nothing had changed. Wife. Dogs. Silence. Shadows.

So why did it feel like the room itself was waiting for something?

He slid out of bed as quietly as he could, bare feet careful on the old floorboards. The dogs didn't stir. His wife shifted once, sighed, and drifted deeper into sleep.

He moved through the hallway like he had a hundred nights before, the kind of movement that should have been muscle memory, harmless, unremarkable.

At the first door he paused, eased it open just enough. His daughter's shape rose and fell beneath her blanket, one hand curled under her cheek. A faint whistle of breath. Perfectly still. Perfectly safe.

At the second door, the same. His son sprawled sideways across the mattress, arms flung out as if sleep had claimed him mid-stride. The tiny night-light painted the room in its soft glow. The boy didn't stir. Not even a twitch.

All normal. Exactly as it should be.

So why did the unease knot tighter with every step?

He leaned against the cool plaster of the upstairs hallway and let his eyes drift to the window. The night outside was the kind he'd known all his life — suburban quiet, the tidy rhythm of houses folded into darkness. The lone streetlamp humming over the sidewalk like a watchman. A sky without stars pressed down, heavy and unbroken.

For a moment, it could have been any night, ordinary and forgettable.

Beyond the glass though, the night sprawled over the neighborhood like a heavy sheet, thick and unmoving. The air itself looked wrong, too dense, as if holding its breath.

He squinted, trying to place what unsettled him — the shadows seemed darker than they should have been, the street beyond the hedges too still.

He pressed a palm against the frame, fingertips buzzing with a sensation he couldn't name.

It was like touching the afterimage of a sound — not vibration, not heat, but something thinner, stranger, as though the wood remembered a scream that had once passed through it.

The house was safe. The family was safe. And yet he couldn't shake the certainty that the night outside was not the same one that had been there when he went to bed.

The thirst struck him all at once, sharp and undeniable, as if something had wrung every drop of moisture from his body while he slept. His tongue clung to the roof of his mouth, his throat parched with a need that felt larger than water.

He rose, moving through the house with the ease of long familiarity — the turns, the doorframes, the way each stair groaned differently underfoot. Yet each sound echoed too long, as though the silence of the place swallowed and reshaped it.

It wasn't the ordinary quiet of a sleeping home. This was a deeper silence, something that pressed into the marrow. It wasn't just around him, but inside him, seeping through his ribs, settling behind his eyes. He felt it disturb something essential, some buried core of himself that recoiled as though it recognized a danger he could not name.

He pressed on, bare feet gliding over old boards, each creak a reminder that the house was alive in ways he didn't entirely trust. The hum of the refrigerator became a low drone, insectile, far away and near at once. He crossed into the kitchen and reached for a glass, the motion both automatic and trembling.

The window above the sink framed the street outside like a painting. Across the way, a single streetlight burned, its pale amber glow bleaching the sidewalk below into an island of artificial day.

Then the night showed him something it shouldn't have.

Just beyond the circle of amber light stood a shape that should have been a man, but wasn't.

It had the outline of a person — shoulders, a head tilted just so. But the way it shifted suggested something wild, undiscovered — a cryptid born of darkness.

The glow from the streetlamp didn't fall on it — the light slid off as if it refused to make contact.

He felt the prickle rise along his arms before his mind caught up. Was it looking at him? He couldn't tell; the "head" had no features he could make out, just suggestions. But a pulse of adrenaline told his body the answer anyway: yes. Yes, it was.

The figure began to move — not walking, not gliding, but a slow drift that was part air and part something else, as though another plane of existence were brushing up against this one.

Its edges blurred, half-smoke, half-substance, and it floated down the block until the dark swallowed it.

He stayed at the window, hypnotized, eyes following the place where it had been.

The streetlight burned steady, the sidewalk empty, but his mind couldn't release the image.

It was as if the darkness itself still carried the afterimage of the shape, burned onto his vision like a phantom sunspot.

He waited, breath shallow, every nerve prickling.

A swirl of emotions rippled through him, stirring the primal brain that spoke in sensations rather than words. Fight or flight was too neat a phrase — it was both at once, each one pulling hard, tearing him in two directions. He felt the raw alertness of prey and the sudden hunger of a predator.

The contradiction made him lightheaded, as though danger had rewired him into something unrecognizable.

Mostly, though, he couldn't move. His body seemed soldered to the floor, gaze locked on the glass, caught in the gravity of the night outside.

A moment later, something flickered at the edge of his vision.

He squinted into the darkness, trying to focus, heart knocking hard against his ribs.

The figure that had drifted left, away from him, now seemed to shimmer on the right — same silhouette, but on his side of the street, as if it had slipped between realities and was drawing closer to his house.

He tried to pin it down, but the more he focused the less certain he was of what he was seeing.

The shadow's outline wavered, became air, then slid again — not across the street this time, but toward the side of the house, disappearing from view.

The subtle unease that had been with him since waking hardened in an instant into panic, adrenaline flooding his system, every instinct shrieking that something was at the edge of his world and now wanted in.

A shiver rattled through him, sudden and bone-deep, and he set the glass down with a clink too loud for the hour. The thought came to him sharp, undeniable: he had to check on everyone. Now.

He moved fast, not running, not yet, but that panicked half-run of a man trying to seem in control.

His feet carried him back upstairs, each step a drumbeat, his breath clipped and shallow.

He reached the first door, shoved it open — The bed was gone.

The whole room was gone.

Where his daughter's posters and toys should have been, there was a desk, a filing cabinet, and stacks of paper.

An office.

His knees wavered. He blinked hard, but the scene didn't change.

"What the hell...?"

He lurched to the next door. His son's room. Only it wasn't.

A wide screen flickered blue, game controllers scattered on a table he'd never seen before. Empty cups, a couch instead of a bed. A stranger's room.

His chest tightened, breath breaking into a ragged yell. "Sarah?" His wife's name cracked the silence. Louder now, rawer: "Sarah!"

He bolted down the hall, no longer caring about noise, skidding into the bedroom doorway.

What met him stopped him cold: the room gutted, ladders leaned against the walls, tarps folded over the bare mattress, paint cans sweating chemical fumes. Renovation, as if their life had been stripped away mid-stroke.

"Sarah!" His voice tore.

He stumbled back, turned, sprinted down the stairs two at a time. Yelling their names over and over until the words broke into noise.

His foot caught on something — a low bench that hadn't been there before. He pitched forward, smacked the floor. Pain flared. "Shit!" The word burst out, then again, louder, a mantra against the madness: "Shit! Shit! Shit!"

He scrambled up, heart slamming, and tore through the downstairs.

The house had turned inside out.

Chairs upended, legs stabbing skyward. The coffee table flipped belly-up. Every frame on the walls hung crooked, reversed, wrong — family photos faced inward to the plaster, artwork twisted into nonsense angles.

He staggered back into the kitchen, sweat slick on his palms. His eyes darted to the window.

The shadow was there. Right there. Inches beyond the glass, as if it had been standing silent, watching his frantic flight through the house.

Slowly, impossibly slowly, the shadow's arm began to rise. The movement was jerky at first, then smooth, as if the air itself resisted and then gave way.

His eyes locked on it, unable to blink, every second stretched into an eternity.

The figure's limb extended upward, then outward, deliberate, mechanical, inexorable.

The finger leveled at him.

It wasn't just a point. It was a verdict. His chest caved under the weight of it, his breath shallow and sharp, as though the pointing had stripped the oxygen from the kitchen itself.

The sensation was layered: accusatory, yes, but more than that. Threatening. Claiming. He felt like a man marked, chosen. The way a repo man doesn't argue or explain, but simply arrives to collect what is already considered gone.

He wanted to shout, to move, to do anything but watch, but the gesture pinned him in place. It was a tether, invisible but strong, holding him in its dark gravity.

His heart pounded a frantic rhythm while his body refused to answer.

The pointing stretched on unbearably long, as though the shadow meant for him to drown in the silence between them, to absorb the truth of his own powerlessness.

Then it faded — not gone, but absorbed, like ink spilling into water.

A cold rolled over him in a wave, a pressure that locked his lungs. Goosebumps erupted so sharp they hurt, ridges of dread rising like mountains under his skin.

The certainty landed in him like a stone dropped down a well: the shadow wasn't outside anymore.

It was in the house.

Heart hammering, he snatched the baseball bat propped against the back door, its familiar weight suddenly alien in his hands.

He moved on instinct, circling the kitchen and front rooms, peeking through blinds and curtains as though the house itself had sprouted eyes.

At the first window, he pulled the slat just enough to see. Street empty. No movement. The streetlight's glow reached only as far as it wanted, stopping short, leaving a black ocean beyond.

He released the slat, moved to the next.

Another window, another frame of nothing.

The hedge line looked wrong, too stiff, like cardboard cutouts of shrubs. He pressed his forehead to the cool glass; it felt colder than it should. His pulse ticked against it like a moth's wings.

He moved again.

Each step louder, his breath a hiss in his ears.

Another window — the alley. Not even the wind stirred there. A plastic bag sat unmoving in a puddle, edges sharp as if frozen mid-flicker. He found himself holding the bat tighter, knuckles aching.

The urge to know pressed at him, an impatience that burned hotter than fear.

He moved toward the back door with a strange confidence, each step quick and sure, as if he had finally decided to confront whatever had chosen him.

The weight of the bat steadied him, lent him the feeling of being armed, ready, righteous.

But the closer he came, the more that confidence thinned.

By the time his hand brushed the deadbolt, the bravado had drained out of him like water slipping down a crack.

His chest tightened, knees light.

He wasn't a hunter approaching prey anymore — he was a child again, trembling at the thought of looking under his bed in the middle of the night.

Finally, he eased the deadbolt, cracked the back door open, and stepped outside.

The air wrapped around him like a wet sheet, cold and damp, clinging to his skin.

He waited for the usual night chorus — crickets, a distant dog, the faint rush of cars on the main road — but nothing came. No chirp, no buzz, no hum. Only the sound of his own breathing and the tiny drip of water from the gutter.

His eyes roamed the neighboring houses.

They stood exactly where they always had, yet they seemed wrong: windows blank and dark, roofs sagging slightly, the siding dull as old bones. Not a flicker of a lamp or a TV glow.

It wasn't just that no one was awake; it was the sense that no one was there. The houses looked like they'd been emptied long ago and left standing as props.

A deep loneliness seeped into him, colder than the air.

The yard stretched out, not as a familiar space but as an island in a dead world. For a flicker of a second he was sure he was the last man alive.

He circled the house, eyes darting into every shadow, nerves pulled taut until they hummed.

Nothing.

Only emptiness, the kind that eats sound.

When he came back in, his hands shook as he slid each deadbolt home, one by one, sealing himself in as if that could help.

He leaned on the bat, muscles trembling, exhaled a breath that felt like it belonged to someone else.

He turned toward the stairs, a grown man thinking of finding some closet to hide in upstairs like a frightened child. The thought barely formed when something inside him snapped tight.

His chest seized, and a storm of emotions crashed through him all at once.

Not just fear — something deeper, heavier.

It was the sense of standing before a force that existed outside the human scale, something that had been here long before him and would remain long after.

His skin prickled as if every hair on his body recognized it before his mind did. His stomach lurched, not with sickness but with the weight of inevitability.

His heart didn't just hammer; it stuttered, as if trying to skip the moment entirely.

The air pressed down, thick and charged, and he knew without knowing that he had stumbled into the presence of something vast and merciless, something that saw him the way a flood sees a drowning man.

The shadow was standing in the hallway.

His body locked, lungs strangled against his ribs.

The shadow loomed larger than the hallway could hold, a darkness where light bent and stopped. Each step it took toward him seemed less a movement than a collapse of space, the inevitability of a fate closing in.

He felt it before he truly saw it: the certainty that this was not something a man could run from.

The shape shifted, peeled.

Not quickly, not mercifully, but with a slowness that made every second ache.

The blackness folded against itself, layer by layer, until suggestion became form. Somewhere in that abyss of spirit, features began to surface.

The longer he stared, the less he trusted his own eyes, and still it resolved.

A face.

His face.

Recognition took forever, a revelation that scraped his mind raw.

First, vague familiarity. Then resemblance. Then the truth: he was looking at himself. His own gray skin, his own wide, unblinking eyes, staring back at him like a reflection dragged out of a void.

The doppelgänger held him there, expressionless, staring for what felt like hours, until time itself seemed to wither.

Then it leaned forward, impossibly slow, foreboding, until he could feel the cold breath graze his ear.

The whisper came, not in any language he knew, but in something older — a dead tongue, spoken once by a people who existed outside of the world, in a time that should never have been.

And yet he understood. He understood every syllable.

At first, a short, nervous laugh escaped him, brittle and out of place. It fluttered in the silence, thin and frantic, before dissolving into a sob.

Tears burned his eyes, spilling hot down his face, the sound raw and helpless. But even that release was stolen from him, cut short as if the very act of crying had been severed at the root, leaving only the hollow weight of what he'd heard.

The meaning finally detonated in him, filling his skull like fire.

His eyes bulged, wild with a crazed determination.

He gripped the bat in both hands, knuckles white, ready not just to defend but to battle, to wage war against this abyss wearing his own face.

With a guttural yell, he swung.

The bat arced through the air and cracked into his own temple.

Pain lanced white-hot, but his scream rose not in agony, but in fury.

He screamed at the shadow, again and again, each swing wilder, each crack louder.

Blood sprayed, a mist across his face and the walls, as splinters leapt from the wood.

His face — the face in the shadow — flickered, blurred, and then dissolved, swallowed back into the dark.

The vanishing wasn't abrupt but deliberate, a slow retreat into nothingness, like a curtain drawn closed at the end of a performance. It carried the finality of a presence finished with its task. It didn't flee. It didn't lose. It simply left, leaving him with the sense that it had accomplished exactly what it came to do.

Still he swung, shrieking like a berserker, smashing himself over and over, blood pouring in sheets down his face and neck. Each blow more violent, more deranged, his voice climbing into a ragged, animal howl.

One final, visceral thrash came down across the crown of his skull, a blow so savage it rattled his teeth and blurred his vision.

The whites of his eyes burst with red as blood vessels popped, his gaze swimming in a haze of crimson.

The pain didn't stay contained — it raced down his spine like a fuse soaked in gasoline and lit aflame, every nerve igniting in a roaring blaze.

The bat shrieked against bone, wood meeting flesh with a wet, splintering crack that filled the room.

The force tore through him and through the bat alike. It split, cracked down its middle, until at last it broke completely, snapping jagged in his hands.

The fat end of the bat tore free, clattering to the floor with a wet thud, landing in the growing pool of blood at his feet. A few strands of hair clung to its splintered edge.

He was left holding the handle — the bottom half — its jagged point jutting upward like a crude spear, slick and trembling in his grip.

He stood there, drenched, streaming crimson, panting in great heaving gasps. Mouth agape, drooling like a rabid animal. Saliva pooled with the blood on the floor. His body trembled, a lunatic warrior carved from blood and rage.

For a long, shuddering moment, he seemed almost triumphant.

Then the rage drained from him, sliding out of his eyes like water down glass. His chest still heaved, but the fire guttered. Silence filled him.

Without a sound, he raised the broken bat.

He stared at it with a blank expression that had never occupied his face even once in his life and a faint flicker of amusement flashed across his face. The jagged end gleamed wet in the kitchen night-light.

He smirked briefly and then with an inhuman suddenness, he drove it hard into his throat, ramming it deep until it burst out in a gout of blood.

A fountain sprayed across the walls, the floor, the ceiling. His body jerked once, twice, then collapsed.

His body lay on the floor twitching grotesquely, legs shooting straight out in rigid spasms as if jolted by some invisible current.

His arms jerked against the tile, hands convulsing, clutching at the air. Fingers curled and uncurled frantically, scrabbling toward nothing, as though they knew there was something just out of reach — some unseen hand, some lifeline — that could pull him back if only he could grasp it.

At last his hands slackened, dropped, and he settled into a lifeless heap.

The bat jutted grotesquely from his neck as the last pulse of blood spread into a black pool beneath him.

The house exhaled into stillness.

Inside, everything was back where it belonged.

The pictures hung straight on the walls again, smiling faces turned outward. The furniture sat patiently in its places, the couch settled, the chairs upright, the coffee table steady on its legs.

Even the air seemed ordinary once more, calm and undisturbed, as though nothing had ever happened at all.

Then came a sound.

A faint creak at the top of the stairs.

Slow, measured footsteps began their descent, wood sighing under the weight.

At the base of the steps a light flickered on, spilling warm yellow just yards from where his body lay mangled in a pool of blood, saliva, and hair — horrific in its stillness.

From the glow, a woman's voice drifted into the night-filled house — gentle, tender — the voice of a devoted wife.

"Dan? Are you okay?"

Jason Garman is a horror writer from the suburbs of Peoria, Illinois. His work leans toward psychological and atmospheric horror, often exploring domestic spaces, identity, and the quiet unease lurking beneath ordinary life. He is currently working on the release of his debut novel, **Reflections in the Dark.**

KILLING TREES

BY BRIAN S ROE

KILLING TREES

BY BRIAN S. ROE

Welcome to Red Oak Farms, a planned community only 45 minutes from downtown Indianapolis! Your new home will combine the quiet and peace of country living with the convenience of being close to one of the Midwest's most vibrant and growing cities. You'll love the wide open lots, gorgeous green spaces, and friendly neighbors of your Red Oak Farm home. And your kiddos will love going to some of the best, and safest, schools in the state! Grocery shopping, convenience stores, and a variety of restaurants are only minutes away. And we're only twenty minutes away from Skybux Casino and Racetrack!

From Red Oak Farms, it's only a ten minute drive to I-74, connect to I-70, and then straight into Indianapolis. Or take 465 to any destination in the Metro Indianapolis area.

Welcome to Red Oak Farms! We've waited so long for you to join us, we know you'll want to stay!

The sun was still huddling under the astern horizon as a cold mist blanketed the fields and neighborhoods of Tucker Township. Gas gurgled into another beat-up can as Mitch held the nozzle and wished he'd thought to wear gloves. The metal handle was far colder than he'd expected and his hand was already cramping by the time he'd filled the five cans. He had an unlit cigarette behind his ear, ready to go the second he plopped back into the truck's seat. Normally, he'd have it hanging off of his lower lip but he didn't want to get any sass from an early riser soccer-mom. He didn't want sass from anybody.

He'd already been into the convenience store that sat beside the pumps for energy drinks, smokes, and jerky. The trucks were topped off with diesel. After this gas can was filled, they could hit the road. Mitch drove the smaller of the two trucks, an old F-250 warhorse that carried the hand tools and crews of Tressler Tree Removal. Even now Juan, Chico, and Tom were asleep in the cab. Manuel drove the newer F-350 and trailer that hauled the excavator and Bobcat. Andre sat shotgun in the 350, sipping coffee and scrolling through his phone. One of these assholes should be out here filling these damned cans, Mitch fumed suddenly. No, ditch that, keep the temper down man. Keep your fucking trouble-making temper down.

Clunk! Finally the pump shut off and Mitch pulled it from the filled can. He replaced the nozzle, stowed the can, and hauled himself into the Ford's cab. Kilink-scritch! went his Zippo as he lit his well deserved Camel. He cupped his hand around the flame for a few seconds to warm some feeling back into it. None of the crew moved as he filled the cab with smoke, started the truck, and began to drive away. He saw Manuel pull the trailer truck in behind him as they drove to today's site.

They drove past cookie-cutter subdivisions full of taupe and putty colored houses as devoid of individuality as office cubicles. This area had been farmland for generations, but now was a breeding ground/feed lot for more and more people. Mitch drove past the sprawling neighborhoods with names like Willow Creek, Maple Trace, and Pine Grove. His boss, Terry Tressler, always made the real estate joke about 'killing the trees and then naming the neighborhood after them. Mitch and his crew were the hired hatchet-men who killed and cleared the trees that made these acres of insipid housing infill possible. It was a job that Mitch did not because he liked it, but because he was allowed to do it. Only Tressler had been willing to give him a chance once he'd gotten out of prison. And if deforesting the entire state was what it took to keep Mitch from going back to prison, well, he'd saw down every damned sapling he came across.

The grove they'd be clearing today wasn't far past the last neighborhood, Shady Elm Place, but it felt somehow far more distant. Like it was a place out of time with the rest of the area. Forgotten somehow – dark, and ignored. They drove down an access road that cut through a stubbled corn field and even this far away there was something strange about the dense woods. Mitch stared at it trying to figure out the optical trick that was making the copse seem so unsettling.

As if reading his mind, Juan answered the visual oddity.

"It's like the sun isn't reaching through those trees. It's going to be cold as fuck in there."

"You'll warm up once you get to working," Mitch said pointlessly. As they pulled the trucks up to the edge of the woods and stopped, the two men in the back started to move around and wake up. Drink cans were shaken to check for dregs and tilted up to catch any remaining nectar. Hoodies were zipped up and cigarettes lit as they disembarked from the trucks like bedraggled soldiers. They all stood for a moment looking at the dense deepness of the woods.

Normally Mitch would have barked to get them started, but he was under the place's spell as much as they were. He felt like he was falling into the dark spaces between the trees, even though he was standing on stable ground. He could feel the tension of the other men around him even though none of them said a word. Screw this, time to get busy.

He started calling out assignments even though this was unnecessary with this crew. These guys had done this job together so many times, they each knew their role of what to do and most importantly, how to stay out of each other's way. When you were dealing with heavy equipment and chainsaws, you had to be very aware of what was going on around you. He'd seen men torn apart by the foolish collision of metal and flesh. Metal always won.

They started by clearing the thin scrub and saplings at the edge of the woods. They needed to make a path to go into the grove to best determine a system for felling and removing the cut trees. Mitch looked over to see Andre in the Bobcat, slicing into the edge of the woods with the brush saw attachment. Manuel and Tom were unloading the excavator from the trailer. The others were oiling and fueling their saws and brushcutters. The groggy morning air of dawn was soon ripped into by the mechanical roars of smoke belching power tools.

Mitch was going over his archaic McCulloch, checking fuel lines and filters. The chainsaw was ancient compared to modern saws, but Terry Tressler believed"It's not how much money you make, but how little you spend that counts." It was his down-home wisdom way of saying that he was a skinflint bastard and Tressler Tree Removal was always the cheapest bidder. Tressler got by with it because he hired men with pasts, men who the rest of the world had thrown away and then gotten pissed at when they came back from the junkyard. Mitch was one of those men. Which gave him great sympathy for the old chainsaw. He knew what it felt like to be thrown away and he didn't want to do it to anyone, or anything else. Plus, once the old saw got going, it was a true fucking monster.

A loud shriek tore through the early morning air. Mitch spun towards it to see that it was just the brush saw on the Bobcat. A sapling had gotten caught against the spinning blade and sounded like a child's scream mixed with a high violin note. He noticed everyone else but Andre had reacted the same way that Mitch had. Why were they all so jumpy?

Drop it, there's work to do. When you overthink things and get too deep in your head, the workday seems to take forever. Get the job done.

As he walked into the woods, Mitch felt a presence in front of him. Not of a person or animal, but of something still, huge and looming. He forced his vision deeper into the gloom and saw a massive burr oak squatting near the center of the woods. This was the tree that Tressler said the developer wanted to name the neighborhood after. But since no one wanted to live in Burr Oak Farms, they'd decided that it was actually a Red Oak. Mitch didn't really care. He was going to cut it down and then it would be hauled off to a sawmill outside of Elwood.

He was struck again by how this small forest seemed far bigger than it really was. It was really only four or five acres, but it seemed to go on forever once you began looking into it. Mitch refocused himself. None of that would matter once they started clearing the bigger trees. It would end up scoured clean, like every other plot they'd worked on. There were houses to build, concrete to pour, asphalt to lay. The land needed to be debrided and then scabbed over with concrete. That was the only way to show the world who was boss.

A soft mist of a thought came into his mind that maybe this place should be allowed to exist as it was. One little space that men would not penetrate. Maybe the world needed some of these deep, quiet places to keep the flow of life going. Was it too much to ask for just this peaceful haven to be left unmolested? If we left now, nothing too bad would happen even though we'd hurt the young trees.

Mitch shook his head to clear it and quickly looked around like he was trying to find someone who had whispered in his ear. What the hell was wrong with him? He was standing there with his saw hanging at his side, having a bullshit mental debate with some trees. He hefted the McCulloch and walked into the woods.

Hours later, the sun had brightened the outside world, but amongst the trees, all was still shade and gloom. The men had made good headway, although they'd been stalled by a dense thicket of honey locusts that ringed the edge of the woods. Honey locusts have dense, stringy wood and are covered in clumps of three-to-four inch thorns that can spike through leather gloves eerily easily. When they're cut, the limbs tend to flail about as if seeking to sink those thorns into eyes or exposed skin.

Mitch had been clearing a ring around the massive burr oak before he attempted the monster itself. It was a full twenty feet in diameter, something he'd never heard of with this species. The trunk seemed to have split at some point and grown back together, leaving the bottom trunk shaped like a massive bowling pin. There seemed to be a deep cavity in it that struck Mitch as a giant mouth or portal. He wondered what rot and filth they'd find inside when they finally felled the great beast of an oak.

He sat on a fresh stump of a maple he'd taken down and ate a few strips of jerky, drank some water, and lit a smoke. He noticed that everything had gone suddenly quiet. All of the saws were stopped, and if the excavator was running, it was far enough away that Mitch couldn't hear it. He breathed in a lungful of Camel smoke and let it out through his nose. Even over the tobacco he could smell the deep, rich loam smell of the woods. Just for that slow single tick of a universal clock, he felt great and a calming peace. Something he'd not felt since childhood, and even then rarely. He didn't bother taking another drag from the cigarette. He just sat there.

A furious scream broke through his solace.

"Fuck man! God fucking damn it!" It was Chico. Mitch dropped the butt and ran towards the group of men.

Chico was holding his right hand as a steady stream of blood was pouring out. Mitch at first assumed he'd cut it off with a saw, but none had been running. The hand didn't look like a saw cut, it looked more like it had been caught in an alligator's mouth and then pulled quickly out.

"It was that fucking honey locust! Damn branch wrapped itself around my arm and squeezed!" His face was glowing with pain and fury. Andre pulled off his hoodie and started to wrap it around Chico's hand.

"Fuck you man!" Chico glared at Andre like a wolf with a leg caught in a trap.

"Whoa, we're cool man. I just need to stop that bleeding, right?" Andre's bass voice rumbled a calming tone. Chico's face stayed feral for a beat and then calmed and it looked like he might cry. Andre got the hoodie wrapped around the hand and forearm and tied the sleeves. Chico was still obviously hurting, but was calming down.

Mitch caught Andre's attention and tossed him the smaller truck's keys.

"There's a drugstore clinic a few miles back. Get him there now." Andre nodded and helped Chico walk out of the woods. Chico wasn't steady and he stumbled several times on the way out. Mitch looked down and was stunned and sickened by the amount of blood on the ground. Mitch had seen his share of blood, but this seemed unreal.

"Honey locusts are real nasty." Manuel said to no one.

"Get back to it. Watch yourselves around those thorns," Mitch said and then walked back to his saw. He suddenly felt afraid and then angry because of having been made afraid. He snatched up the McCulloch and pulled on the starting cord like he was trying to rip it out of the saw. The motor caught eagerly and roared out Mitch's anger.

He strode to the old oak and tore the spinning edge of the chain into the dense bark of the tree. He had no plan, was not making smart cuts, was just wanting to rip into this giant damned monster that sat like a squatting god surrounded by its worshipping cult. Mitch cut a chaotic circle around the perimeter of the oak. He realized that he wasn't trying to cut it down. He was trying to hurt it.

By the time he had worked his way fully around the tree, he was panting and his eyes goggled in their sockets. Even his mighty McCulloch had done little more than scratch the outside of the bark. He needed to calm down, be smart and have a plan. He stared at the dark opening at the front of the tree and decided that's where he'd make his cut. The wood on that side should be thinner so he wouldn't have to go as deep to fell the damned thing. He eyed his fall-line to make sure no one else was in the path of the soon to fall tree. He didn't see, or hear anyone. Fine, whatever, he didn't care right now. He had a task and was still pissed off and worked up.

His first deep cut felt glorious. The saw bit cleanly and the motor roared powerfully. He managed to take out a wedge about two feet deep. The wood smelled moist and strong, not rotten at all. He didn't care. This tree could live another hundred years, but today was its last. Mitch revved the McCulloch and cut in again.

The blade hit something that nearly killed the motor. Mitch immediately powered down the saw, afraid of kickback. He worked the saw free and looked over the cut. There seemed to be white stone chips in the sawdust and on the saw's blade. Perplexed, Mitch checked the blade and seeing that it still felt sharp, started the saw and began a cut in a new place. He again reached the same depth as before when the saw hit something hard. This time, the motor died.

The blade also had bent and dulled teeth. Mitch cursed and strode back to the 250 to get another. As he walked up to the trucks he realized that no one else was around.

"Hey!" he bellowed. "Manuel! Tom! Where the hell are you assholes?!" No response. Great. Just what he needed. His crew were off getting high while he did the work. He grabbed several new blades and another, larger saw. He'd at least get that oak to come down. Then when he found those lazy punks, he'd fire all of them.

New blade installed, gas refilled, saw checked and primed. Instead of making deep felling cuts, Mitch worked around the opening in the trunk to see what was inside of it. It obviously wasn't wood and he didn't feel like having the saw kickback into his chest and leave him to bleed out alone in the woods. He went from being a butcher to being a surgeon, cutting precisely and avoiding the hard mass within the wood. He cut like this for a solid hour before he finally broke through the layer covering the cavity within.

He looked inside and saw a pale arm. Not a human arm, more like a doll's arm. It was a statue. He went back to the truck to get a large crowbar. He didn't even think to wonder about where the rest of his crew was. His mind was completely focused on the tree.

He pried away bark and wood until he made an opening in the split trunk. As he gave one final strong push against the crow bar, a small avalanche of stone and concrete poured from the hole. Statues, some the size of dolls, some the size of small children, toppled out. And headstones. Infant headstones. Mitch's brain knew what he was seeing, but he couldn't comprehend what it might mean. He just stared at the pile of chipped and broken things that now lay at his feet. He stared at it and tried to force his mind to make sense of it. He began to focus on individual bits instead of the whole. There was a geode, unsplit. Several chert spearheads that still looked sharp enough to cut. Statues of children and angels. Flat stones with odd stars carved into them. And something that looked very much like a flute made of stone.

Mitch fell backwards and sat with a thud in the leaf litter. His mind was not yet gone, but was going. He knew that this was strange, but a part of him also knew it shouldn't be hitting him this hard. He felt like he was being drugged, but on a psychic level. His mind began to quickly retreat into a memory of his grandmother on a cold autumn night. She was telling him about feather crowns.

"You see, when somebody dies, their soul'll go out of their head and make these little crowns out of the feathers in their pillow. It's like the force of their soul leaving weaves, a bunch of feathers into this little, flat crown. When my momma died, I cut her pillow open and she had three crowns in there. Most folks you're lucky to find one. But my momma was special."

A whispering presence was again in his mind. It told him that it was too late and that he would pay a price for what he'd done.

Mitch suddenly felt very afraid, like he was standing on the absolute edge of an impossible cliff and the wind was blowing against his back, trying to push him over.

There was something ancient and strong at work here, something that existed long before mankind ever did. Something that early settlers to this part of the world had made a deal with. A deal that Mitch might just have undone. He wished so hard that his Grandma was here right now. She'd know what to do. She was a clever woman, like her momma. Mitch wasn't clever. He was just a dumb, angry man who did dumb, angry things. He was choke-sobbing now as he flipped himself forward to rest on all fours. He knew he must look like a crazy person, but he didn't care.

Maybe he could fix things! He bolted upright and began scooping the stone detritus back into the tree. He tried to put it in somehow respectfully, as if his obedient actions could undo the mistake he'd made. He made sure that every single bit was retrieved and replaced. By the time he was finished he was panting and smiling an empty idiot's grin. He looked at the tree hopefully, tears streaming from his eyes, like an abused child hoping for a hug instead of a backhand. He heard someone coming through the woods behind him, but he didn't care. He had to make sure he was okay with the tree.

A sound like great, dry snakes sliding through underbrush rustled through his sobs.

Long, rope-like limbs covered in thorns, streaked through the leaves and wrapped around him. They were massive whips, cracking at his flesh and ripping through his clothes. The pain was so sharp that he thought he was going to black out. But it also made him feel the flagellant's joy of being punished for his trespasses. The branches sawed into him with blades made of bark and thorns. He bled his crimson sacrifice onto the oak's hungry roots.

A large branch covered in massive spikes smacked into his back and propelled him towards the damaged gap of the tree. The branch swatted him over and over, tearing out gobbets of bloody flesh as he was corralled into the dark chasm. He saw that the thorn trees were just appendages of the massive oak, and it was using them to destroy him.

The last thing he knew before he fell into blood black oblivion, was that the inside of the tree was covered in hard, dark honey locust thorns.

Brian S. Roe lives in an ancient hunting shack surrounded by dying and arcane trees. His cat-friend Athena keeps the goblins and pixies under control.

LITTLE CIRCLES

BY ANN O'MARA HEYWARD

LITTLE CIRCLES

BY ANN O'MARA HEYWARD

I woke at 3 a.m. again, struggling, swaddled in sheets soaked in my own sweat. I had no fucking idea why I'd been having the dream. Night after goddamn night. For weeks.

In my dream, I am small, held securely in someone's arm, peering at a piece of paper on a desk below. Neat columns of little circles marching down the page. I watch, as a woman's hand holds a pen, and fills in some of the circles, turning them black. Filling them in carries some desperate importance. Inevitably, I wake at that point in a panic, drenched and chilled.

I thought about asking my sister if the dream made any sense to her. I don't remember our parents at all; I only know they're gone. We were raised by the state, in one of the homes set up in the late twenties. Until my sister turned ten, we were together. They kept siblings together if they were little, but at ten, we went separate ways as boys and girls. I was two years younger. I missed her when she left for the girls' dormitory. I still saw her from time to time; the girls began performing their tasks at ten, the cleaning and cooking and gardening and laundry that an institution housing hundreds of children required, along with helping to care for the babies and little ones. As a boy, my tasks were different. We spent a few hours a day at our desks, first learning to read and write and calculate, then learning how to ask the AI to do those things for us. But it wasn't all sitting at our desks. We were assigned our own tasks to keep the place going: fixing things, mending fences, learning to shoot, to drive, raising and lowering the flag at sunrise and sunset, learning to stand watch for hours along the fence line.

I loved watching the flag ripple and snap in the wind – especially the way the stars would appear, then disappear, then appear again as the fabric was pulled this way and that – but it was never clearly explained to us exactly what we were watching for.

When I saw my sister after she joined the girls, she was wearing the ankle length dresses and aprons that they all wore. As she went about her duties, we would occasionally get the chance to talk briefly. I told her about everything I was learning – the reading, the writing, the fractions I struggled with, and later, my talks with the AI – and she listened in wonder and admiration. They had no school. Their work filled their entire day, until after hundreds of dishes were cleaned and put away after dinner, and the kitchens prepared for breakfast. By then they were happy just to sleep, after the matron heard their prayers.

It wasn't much different from any kid's upbringing in a regular household with parents. Boys went to school and learned to do man-things; girls stayed at home and learned to do woman-things. More chores for us at the group home, maybe.

Sara , my sister, lived not too far away from where I did, with her husband, Joshua. If I wanted to see her, I needed to go to their place. I was never sure that Joshua was glad to see me, but I thought Sara and the kids would be. It had been too long. Months.

I pulled up in front of their house. It was a nice place, a four-bedroom ranch on a block with others just as nice. I think they call the style Mid Century Modern Revival or something. Josh made good money as an accountant; he's also president of the local businessmen's club. Their place looked like it always did, like their neighbors' did – well tended, lawn green, Josh's SUV in the driveway, toys all over the yard.

The first surprise came when Joshua, then Sara, stepped onto their front porch. How pregnant Sara was. It really had been months since I'd seen her last, and I guess they'd been busy.

But I thought to myself, *Again? Holy shit.* Josh and Sara have five kids already. This one'll be number six. That's not unusual, really. Most of the guys I work with have at least four kids, if they were married. The government incentives are pretty good for each kid, and they increase with each kid you have. I could tell by looking at her, though, that it was starting to wear on Sara, having a kid pretty much once a year since she married Josh at eighteen. She's only twenty-five, but she looked older than Josh, who's thirty-two. And she was too fucking thin, especially for a pregnant woman. The reason for *that* became apparent when she threw her apron over her shoulder for modesty while she helped the latest kid cradled in her arm – *Micah*, I remembered, after a minute's thought, *the youngest is Micah* – find her breast.

Joshua stepped forward to shake my hand.

"Hey, good to see you, man." He always smiled, but it never reached his eyes, somehow. He always looked wary, guarded, like I was going to slip him a three-dollar bill, or take something from him when he's not looking. I smiled back, anyway. To keep seeing Sara, I needed to stay on good terms with Josh. It was his household, after all.

"Hey, look at you," I said to Sara. I meant it to sound affectionate, teasing, but it came out sounding a little shocked, even to me. She reddened, embarrassed by her bulging stomach, glanced involuntarily at Josh... who tried to paint a coat of jovial bro-speak over his displeasure that I was there and interrupting their family routine.

"So, what brings you out, buddy?"

"Just wanted to talk over some old times with my favorite sister," I said, lightly. "I can't stay long."

Josh looked pleased for the first time in the whole conversation. "Well, have a nice visit," he said. "Gotta go Zoom with a client."

Sara and I sat down on the porch swing. My nieces and nephews settled in around us. Rebecca, the oldest at six, the bossy older sister; Mary, the four-year-old, crooned to a doll wrapped in a tiny blanket held to her chest in imitation of Sara holding Micah. Elijah and little Joe, three and two, pushed toy cars back and forth.

I told her about the dream. She frowned, her brow furrowed, and again, I found myself thinking *she looks older than she really is*. She glanced around her as if checking to see who was nearby. Nobody was, except for the kids. A woman walked by on the sidewalk, pushing a stroller and trailed by three kids, one with a dog on a leash. She looked exhausted. Sara lifted her hand

and waved, the woman waved back and kept walking. Sara waited until the woman was another house-length away before she whispered a question.

"Does the name Ethan Stone mean anything to you?" I shook my head.

"You were too little," she said, still speaking in a whisper, "when it all happened. I don't remember all of it myself. But he was killed. Killed on some television show. After that, everything changed."

"How?" I asked her, whispering myself.

"I still don't know why, but one day the police came to the house and got Mom and Dad, and we never saw them again. You and I went to the state home."

I remembered none of this. My earliest memories were after we were already at the state home. I didn't remember Mom and Dad. I said as much to Sara.

"What did they do?" I asked her. "To be arrested, I mean."

She shook her head, as puzzled as I was. "I don't know."

Rebecca, unnoticed by either of us, slipped inside the house.

Both of us were surprised when Joshua stepped onto the porch, his face flushed and clearly angry. He grabbed Sara's arm and hauled her to her feet. Sara looked at me, stunned and bewildered. She didn't speak but I read her face clearly. *What did I do?*

"This visit is over," said Joshua. "Rebecca says you're sitting here whispering secrets."

Sara tried to defend both of us. "No, Joshua, no. Just talking about our childhood."

"You mean your criminal parents?" he sneered. "Get in the house. I'll deal with you in a minute."

"Hey," I started to say, but Sara shook her head at me and went inside. Josh followed her.

I stood there, not sure what to do next. I reached down and ruffled Rebecca's hair. She looked up at me, calmly. "Mommy's getting her punishment now." Her voice was completely matter of fact. She might have said *the sky is blue*, her tone was so serene.

Sweet Jesus Christ.

A minute later, Joshua reappeared and stared at me through the screen. "You can leave, or you can stand there and listen. It makes no fucking difference whatsoever to me." Then he walked away into the interior of the house, unbuckling and pulling his belt from his pants. I stood for a moment more, shaking with rage and shame, then heard the *crack* of the belt hitting my sister's flesh.

Crack.

Crack.

That's when I heard Sara start screaming, begging Joshua to stop.

I couldn't stand there any longer. The Mance Doctrine and the Castle Doctrine, combined, meant Joshua could legally kill me if I tried to intervene. We were taught that in school. Mance says any male has the legal right to manage his household as he sees fit without fear of prosecution or government interference. Castle says he has a right to kill any intruder. I had come to visit, unarmed. Joshua was not.

And I couldn't stand to listen anymore. Even to bear witness. Who would I have borne witness to, anyway? It wasn't a crime.

I got in my car and drove away. I don't think I'll ever see Sara again.

So I had two clues that cost my sister a beating and me, my self-respect: my parents' arrest, and Ethan Stone. I still had no idea what either one meant in terms of my dream. The only Ethan Stone I knew of was a statue of a young guy with a thick head of hair and a shit-eating grin, in the town square. I wouldn't have thought a statue could *have* a shit-eating grin, but it does. The only reason I even knew it was a statue of him is that the base said so.

Ethan Stone. Never forget.

I knew I couldn't ask my nano-AI at home about my parents' arrest, and I was reluctant to ask about Stone, even though he must have been famous to have been on a national television show when he was killed. Not to mention having a statue. Then I remembered exactly where his statue stood, as if he himself was leading me to the answer. With that shit-eating grin.

It was in front of the library.

A week later, I had my permit to visit the library. It wasn't hard to get one. I met all the requirements (*Male*, Y; *Citizen*, Y; *European ancestry*, Y; *Registered resident of library location*, Y; *No arrests or convictions*, Y.)

Just inside the front door, I presented my permit to the guy at the admissions desk. He scrutinized it, scanned my ID, took my photo, and collected my thumbprint. After all that, he asked me what my purpose in visiting was. "Historical research," I answered.

"What era?" he countered.

"Contemporary," I told him, and smiled politely. He thawed a little and rolled his eyes.

"Glad you're not one of those guys who want to read about World War Two or the Civil War." I told him, truthfully, that I'd never heard of either of those things. "You'll be fine, then," he said, and unlocked the inner door.

That smell. I remembered it. From so long ago. I must have been brought to the library, and brought here often, to have that smell be imprinted so firmly. But I had no memory of that either.

It had been a long time since I'd seen a book with paper pages. There were hundreds neatly arranged on shelves, all behind locked glass doors. The cases themselves were arranged around a desk in the center of the room.

I approached the man at the desk. "I'd like to learn more about Ethan Stone," I said.

He looked pleased. "A national hero. We have an excellent collection of material by and about him, in both audio and print," he said, and led me to that section of shelves. He unlocked a glass door and slid it aside. "If I can help you further, don't hesitate to ask."

An hour later, having skimmed four books, listened to a half-dozen audio recordings of Stone's podcasts, and watched the video of his assassination, I was back at the desk. The librarian looked up at me and smiled warmly, as if we were now old friends. "What can I help you with?"

I smiled back, even though my stomach felt like it was filled with a collection of very sharp ice crystals. "The history of the Mance Doctrine, please."

If anything, he looked even happier at my response and practically bounced out of his chair. "Right this way."

An hour after that I had answers to questions it never even occurred to me to ask.

I'm ashamed to admit that. But who *does* question what's normal? Once it becomes that way?

Why was I taught to read, when Sara was not? Why did couples have so many kids? Why does every woman I see wear a long dress and an apron? And why didn't I *see* women that often? Because they mostly stayed behind the closed doors of homes ruled by their husbands or their fathers or their sons?

Stone's following had been mostly men my age. The books said they felt purposeless, ignored, disrespected. They didn't blame themselves. They blamed women.

Choices, Stone said, *ruined everything*. And then a woman killed him.

Mance came along with a simple answer. *Take away all the choices*, he said. *Everything becomes so easy then.*

I think, now, that my dream was about the last election. It was in the twenties, not long after Stone was killed. I was two. The last thing I asked the guy at the library desk to help me find were the news accounts from that year. I didn't think I'd find anything specific about my parents' arrests, and

I was right. There were *thousands* of arrests that year. There hasn't been an election since.

I think my mother was arrested for voting, and my father was arrested for letting her.

The little circles? They were choices.

Ann O'Mara Heyward is a horror fiction and nonfiction writer in Cleveland, Ohio. Her short story "The Carny" won The Ghost Story's Supernatural Fiction Award (Spring 2023) and was nominated for a Pushcart Prize. Her fiction has appeared in anthologies from Solar Press, Hellbound Books, Undertaker Books, Wyrd Harvest Press, Inkd Publishing, RDG Press, and other independent publishers in the US, Australia, and the UK, and has been aired by the No Sleep and Tales to Terrify podcasts. She is also at work on a nonfiction book entitled The Thinking Woman's Guide to Horror Movies, *and co-edited* Hellbound Highway: Anthology of Traveling Terror *for Hellbound Books. Her short story collection,* No One Heard Her Screams, *will be available May 1, 2026. You can find her at www.annoheyward.com and on Facebook at www.facebook.com/AnnOHeyward.*

BLACK HEART OF THE MALL

BY D L WINCHESTER

BLACK HEART OF THE MALL

BY D.L. WINCHESTER

LeRoy Knatt stood at the luggage claim, waiting for the bags to start down the chute.

He noticed a couple of women a short distance away giving him the stink eye. "I'm glad I don't have to vacuum the cow shit off the carpet," one of them said, just loud enough for him to hear.

For a moment, he considered responding, telling them they couldn't enjoy their steak without some cow shit on boots, but decided against it. Hell, they were probably vegetarian, or vegan, or whatever the hell the latest fad was.

Besides, these were his good boots. The ones covered in cow shit were a thousand miles away, back on the Bar-K.

Not for the first time, he wondered how his twin could live in a place like this. Denver pretended to be a western city, but it was just like any other metropolis. Larry had a house in the suburbs, worked in one of the downtown high-rises, and took advantage of the golf courses and ski resorts about half as often as he should.

"Uncle LeRoy!" He heard a voice yell.

The girl came flying toward him, blonde braids flying behind her, a big grin showing a pair of missing teeth. She jumped into his arms, and he pulled her in for a hug.

"Bridget! I swear you get prettier every time I see you!"

"Don't be a liar, Uncle LeRoy."

"It's the God-honest truth," he replied. "How old are you now, five?"

She rolled her eyes. "I just turned *nine,* Uncle LeRoy."

"That's why you're so heavy!" He teased, setting her down and extending his hand to greet her father, who'd finally caught up.

"You shouldn't take off like that, Bridget," Larry scolded. Bridget looked at LeRoy and rolled her eyes as her father ignored the handshake and went for a hug. "It's been too long, brother."

"Just a couple years," LeRoy replied. "I keep telling y'all to come up to the Bar-K for a week or two."

Larry chuckled as they separated. "Tori wouldn't survive the trip. She still hasn't forgiven you for teaching Bridget to shoot a gun on your last visit."

LeRoy couldn't help but notice the differences between him and his brother. Instead of a pearl snap shirt and pressed jeans, Larry wore a button down and slacks. A cell phone was on his belt, and he carried the worried look of a man afraid the world could go on without him.

But the face was almost the same one LeRoy saw every morning in the mirror, blue eyes and brown hair. Larry's was filled out a bit more, his bronzed skin from a tanning bed rather than the Montana sun.

With a buzz, bags started sliding down the chute onto the conveyor. The waiting crowd surged forward, but LeRoy held back. The bags would come out the same no matter where he stood, and he didn't see the sense in being jostled and bumped to get his suitcase a few seconds quicker.

Bridget looked up at him. "I *told* Mama we should come visit you, and she said it sounded absolutely *miserable.*"

LeRoy chuckled. "Hell, it ain't that bad. We just got satellite internet and an indoor water closet!"

She wrinkled her nose. "What's a water closet?"

"A toilet, Bridget," her dad explained.

"What'd you do before then?" she asked.

"Ever hear of an outhouse?" The crowd around the carousel was thinning, and LeRoy spotted his bag. Stepping in, he pulled it off the conveyor and went back to where Bridget and Larry were waiting.

"I think you're pulling my leg," Bridget announced.

"Come up and see it sometime. I'll give it a fresh coat of paint, just for you." With a smile, he scooped her up in his free arm, and they headed toward the door.

LeRoy couldn't sleep.

Something was wrong, though he couldn't put his finger on exactly *what.*

The noise was different. His brother's neighborhood backed up to a railroad, and the trains going by every so often shook the house. Car lights came through the guest room window, too. Even looking up at the sky, it was too bright, the light pollution drowning out the stars.

But it was more than that, a feeling, the kind of thing he couldn't quite put his finger on.

He sighed again. How in the hell could his brother live like this? LeRoy felt compressed, compacted, like the world was closing in around him.

Maybe that was why he felt uneasy?

No, it was deeper than that. Something was wrong with this place, and it bugged him that he couldn't figure out what.

"Rise and shine, sleeping beauty."

"What?" Bridget rubbed her eyes. "What time is it?"

"Time to get up!" LeRoy replied. "We've got to milk the cows, water the horses, and gather the eggs."

"Uncle LeRoy, we don't do that stuff here," Bridget grinned at him.

"How about breakfast? Do you do breakfast?"

She nodded.

"Well, get dressed, and we'll go get something to eat."

While he waited, LeRoy scrawled a note for his brother, letting him know where him and Bridget were.

"Can we get pancakes?" Bridget asked when she came into the kitchen.

"I don't see why not," LeRoy replied with a smile.

The pancake house was in the middle of a shopping center's parking lot. Across the road, a line of fast-food restaurants provided sustenance for folks who couldn't be bothered to leave their cars.

A waitress put a pile of pancakes covered in whipped cream and chocolate syrup in front of Bridget. LeRoy watched her eyes light up as the waitress put a plate of bacon, eggs, and hash browns in front of him.

"Dig in," he encouraged her.

Bridget picked up her fork. Over her shoulder, LeRoy noticed a blonde man with bright red skin and black eyes.

What?

When he looked again, the man's skin was pale, nothing remarkable about him. LeRoy shook his head to clear it. Lack of sleep was getting to him.

"Uncle LeRoy?"

"What? Sorry."

Bridget smiled. "I asked if we could go to the mall today."

"Sure, I don't see why not." He took a bite of his eggs and almost spit them out. They were rubbery and stale, with no flavor. When you were used to eating eggs fresh from the barnyard, this was a step down. "We'll go after breakfast."

The girl giggled. "Uncle LeRoy, it's barely six o'clock. The mall doesn't open until ten."

"Oh, ten, sure," he said, taking a chance on the bacon. It was good. Granted, it was hard to screw up bacon, but it could be done. "What do you want to do until then?"

If he'd thought he was out of place at the airport, the looks he got at the park near his brother's house were even worse. Men and women in athletic gear jogged past, staring at his jeans and boots.

LeRoy didn't care... and decided he couldn't care. He'd be looking at them just as funny if they showed up on his ranch dressed like they were.

He was sitting on a bench at the playground, watching Bridget on the swings, when Larry took a seat next to him and offered him a travel mug of coffee.

"How'd you know we were here?" LeRoy asked.

Larry nodded at Bridget. "The mall doesn't open until ten."

LeRoy chuckled, then narrowed his eyes. Past Bridget, he'd swear one of the joggers had the same red skin he'd seen in the diner. But when he looked back, it was just a bad fake tan.

"I bet she's got a list for you," Larry said.

"Aw, hell," LeRoy replied. "I've had two years to save up."

Another girl ran onto the playground, and LeRoy turned to watch her. Bridget seemed to know her, and soon they were playing together.

Hell, maybe they didn't know each other. Kids were like that, friends before they knew each other's names. LeRoy glanced across the playground to where the girl's mother had taken a seat, and found a pair of black eyes staring back at him.

"Shit!" The coffee fell to the ground, the lid popping open and spilling the liquid everywhere.

Larry chuckled. "You ain't gotta spill it just because it's better than the crap you usually drink."

"Sorry," LeRoy bent and picked up the cup, stealing a look at the woman. She was just a normal suburbanite, normal eyes, normal skin.

Maybe he needed a nap before they headed to the mall.

LeRoy found a space for his rental car in the mall parking lot just after it opened. Bridget had told him which store to park at, and he hadn't asked questions, but when they walked in, she took a folded piece of notebook paper from her pocket.

"Let me see that," LeRoy said, taking it from her.

It was a list of stores, each with a list of items beneath the name.

The list Larry had warned him about.

LeRoy chuckled. "How long have you been working on this?"

"A couple weeks," Bridget admitted.

He read through the list again. "This is pretty impressive," LeRoy said. "I've seen rodeos with less planning than this."

She took the list back from him. "I'm glad you like it."

Already, the rush of people around him was annoying LeRoy. You didn't have to be in a hurry, even in a place like this. At least Bridget was being calm, standing next to a rack of ladies unmentionables waiting for him to get his bearings.

"Well, I don't think this is going to get any less crowded," he said, taking his niece's hand. "Lead the way."

As they walked through the perfume and jewelry, it happened again. A woman, red skin, black eyes, but when he looked again, she was normal.

"Sample, sir?"

He turned to face the salesman, and felt his jaw drop. It was the same thing, but up close.

It was terrifying.

The skin seemed to droop and sag, creating strange shadows on the man's face, and the black eyes were all black, no obvious iris or cornea, like his cows back home.

"What...What..." LeRoy stammered.

"It's cologne, Uncle LeRoy," he blinked, and it was a normal man staring at him. Graying hair, pale skin, blue eyes.

Bridget squeezed his hand. "You okay?"

"Yeah, sorry, just a little tired." He smiled at the salesman. "No, thank you on the sample. I've used the same brand for years."

Bridget pulled him away before the salesman could reply. "I know you're from the country, but surely you know about cologne," she said, leading him into the hall of shops. "First store's over here."

They went into a clothing store where pop music blasted from the speakers. LeRoy followed Bridget, taking items as she handed them to him.

"Won't you outgrow this by tomorrow?" He asked.

She shook her head. "I'm getting some things a size too big so I can grow into them. That way if you don't come back for another two years, I'll be okay."

He couldn't help but chuckle. At her age, the only time him and Larry weren't in t-shirts and shorts were the Sunday expeditions to town for Church. If his mom had turned him loose in a store like this, or any store, really, he'd have been clueless.

In the concourse, he heard a scream.

Heads turned, and Bridget grabbed his hand. "What was that, Uncle LeRoy?"

Another scream, closer. LeRoy looked around and saw a girl not much older than Bridget pointing at a red-skinned *thing* wearing a store nametag. Before LeRoy could do anything, it grabbed the screaming girl and stuffed her in its mouth, skin and jaw stretching to accommodate the child.

"Jesus fucking Christ!" LeRoy realized he was the one that screamed this as pandemonium broke out around them. Bridget tried to run, pulling him, but he held her hand tight. Outside the store, the mall would be a madhouse.

In front of him, the creature finished its meal, its once-skinny frame sagging from the added weight. It turned to face LeRoy and grinned.

LeRoy wished he hadn't left his pistol back at the ranch. This was a problem that required the metric system—nine whole millimeters, to be precise.

The thing took a step toward LeRoy and Bridget, now alone in the store. There was a baseball bat on one of the displays, and LeRoy grabbed it.

It took another step toward him, and LeRoy stepped into a swing, feeling the bat make contact with the thing's skull with a sickening *crack*. The head pulled away from the body, the skin of the neck the only thing that seemed to hold it in place. Then the head rebounded back, and LeRoy took another swing.

The skull flew out of the skin, slamming into a cash register and sending money flying. Dark sludge splattered the clothes and walls. In front of him, the creature's body slumped to the ground, a mound of skin and bone around whatever was left of the thing's last meal.

"Uncle LeRoy?" Bridget, crying, grabbed his leg. "I'm scared."

"That ain't a bad thing, kid," LeRoy said. The bat had snapped in two, obviously more of a prop than an actual weapon. He'd need to find a weapon. "Problem is, to keep being scared, we gotta stay alive."

He moved to the front of the store, standing by the door and staring out into the mall. LeRoy could see them among the crowd, red bodies standing out. How many were there?

A security guard ran by, and LeRoy yanked him into the store. "Where are you going?" He demanded.

"It's every man for himself," the guard replied. "I'm getting out of here!"

LeRoy fought the urge to roll his eyes. "Do you have a weapon?"

"What? Yeah."

He held out a hand. "You won't be needing it."

The guard hesitated, then unholstered a pistol and put it in LeRoy's hand, followed by two spare magazines.

"I'd go out the back," LeRoy started, but the man was running again, right into the cologne salesman.

"Fuck." LeRoy jammed the spare magazines into his pocket, took aim, and fired. The guard tumbled to the floor as the salesman's sludge splattered across the entrance to the department store. Without looking back, the guard disappeared inside.

"What do we do now?" Bridget asked.

LeRoy nodded toward the back of the store. "There'll be a hall back there. Let's use it."

The first room they found was the abandoned security office. LeRoy swung the door closed, testing the locks and finding them sturdy.

If the things could get through that, they were fucked anyway.

A wall of TVs showed him a mall devoid of its usual crowd, the only things still inside are the creatures shuffling along the corridors.

Reports of a disturbance at Denver Park Mall...

LeRoy snapped his head around to see a TV turned to a local news station. The reporter was outside the same door they'd come in, looking serious. Behind her, LeRoy could see folks milling about the parking lot, probably still trying to figure out what had happened.

Then, behind the reporter, the doors opened, and the things started spilling out.

For a moment, the reporter stood there, shocked, watching as the things got closer and closer.

"Run, you idiot! Run!" Bridget yelled at the TV. The camera dropped, becoming a live, jiggling feed of asphalt and painted lines. Then the perspective changed, rising off the ground, before pointing straight down the maw of one of the creatures.

LeRoy switched off the TV. All it told him was they were in deep shit.

"What's that, Uncle LeRoy?" Bridget pointed at one of the screens. He was so proud of her for not panicking, for adapting to the situation.

LeRoy leaned in for a closer look. There, in the center of the food court, surrounded by several of the creatures, was a massive black beating heart.

It looked to be the size of a moving truck. He didn't know how they got it in there, or how he'd missed it the first time he looked. But LeRoy figured if he could destroy it, he might be able to end this.

He started throwing open cabinets and yanking open drawers, looking for anything he could use.

"What are you doing?" Bridget asked.

"Getting ready to fight." LeRoy pulled open a safe under one of the tables, and found three more guns and a pile of magazines. Setting the guns on the table, he pulled out magazines and stuffed them in his pockets.

"Can I fight?"

He shook his head. Taking one of the guns, he handed it to Bridget. "You remember what I taught you last time?"

She nodded.

"Lock the door behind me. If any of the creatures come in here, blow their head off."

"But why aren't you going to wait with me?" Bridget asked.

"Because I think I can end this," LeRoy looked at the screen again. Would a bullet be enough to stop a heart like that? Would it even penetrate it? He studied a map of the mall on the wall, then grinned.

Between him and the food court was a massive sporting goods store. Most of them had stopped selling guns, but still had hunting supplies.

And it gave him an idea.

"Lock the door behind me," he ordered as he started undoing the locks.

Bridget wrapped her arms around him, and LeRoy realized she was crying. "Be careful, Uncle LeRoy."

"I will be, honey. I'll be back before you know it."

LeRoy crouched at the food court entrance. There were maybe a dozen of the creatures surrounding the black heart.

Next to him was a wagon with four five-gallon buckets containing the mall's entire supply of target explosive. It was an interesting com-pound—about the only way to set it off was to shoot it. Usually, it was used in small quantities, though internet videos showed what it could do to things like feral pigs and washing machines.

He hoped it would do a number on the heart.

He just had to get it close enough first.

LeRoy peeked around the corner again. A dozen against one wasn't great odds, but he doubted they would improve.

Besides, the creatures didn't have guns.

He took a deep breath, then entered the food court at a dead run.

Three, four, five of the things went down before any of them reacted, heads exploding and scattering the food court with the sludge. LeRoy kept firing, and saw another go down, then another.

Seven down, five left.

Something grabbed his arm, and he dropped the gun as he was lifted into the air.

Where did this one come from?

He barely managed to get his backup out, but before LeRoy could fire, he heard a gunshot. The creature dropped him, and the fall to the floor knocked the wind out of LeRoy.

There were two more shots, then a scream.

LeRoy forced himself to his feet to find one of the creatures dangling Bridget over its mouth.

Why the fuck is she here?

The gun came up without him thinking about it, and he fired. Bridget fell, twisting to land on her side.

LeRoy saw the last two creatures approaching her, one from each direction. He fired, hitting the first one, then pivoting to the second. It was close, almost too close.

Its head exploded, sending a cloud of sludge into the air.

Bridget turned and grinned at him.

"Come on, we've got to finish this!" he yelled, running for the wagon.

Is this too much? Are you going to bring down the roof?

He stopped.

Hundreds of the creatures were swarming through the corridors, heading toward the food court.

Fuck fuck fuck!

He had to be fast.

LeRoy grabbed one of the barrels and sprinted to place it next to the beating black heart. Running toward Bridget, he scooped her up and ducked behind the counter of one of the restaurants as creatures started appearing in the food court entrance. Dropping the magazine, he slammed a fresh one into the gun, aimed, and fired.

Ka-BOOM!

The shockwave sent him sliding across the tile floor, crashing into equipment. Bridget was crouched behind the counter, her fingers in her ears.

Now that he noticed, his ears were ringing.

There was black sludge everywhere, and a soft tinkle from out in the food court.

The skylight.

He got to his feet, peering out over the counter. The army of approaching creatures was dead, lying lifeless at the entrance to the food court. They were covered in black sludge.

The explosive had done a number on the heart. All that was left was a dark spot on the floor. Everything else had been scattered, along with the tables and chairs.

I'm glad I only used one of those buckets...

LeRoy started laughing.

"What the hell, Uncle LeRoy?" Bridget demanded, getting to her feet.

"That's it, Bridget," he stammered. "We were this close," he held up two fingers, "to your Uncle LeRoy blowing us straight to hell."

He kept laughing, until finally he was laughed out, and collapsed back to the floor again.

Bridget took a piece of paper out of her pocket, and LeRoy realized it was the list. She unfolded it, studied it, and sighed.

"I guess we'll have to save this for another day."

Turns out, LeRoy was not laughed out.

***

D.L. Winchester lives in the foothills of southern Appalachia. A former mortician, his work searches the darkness to find tales worth telling. He is the author of over three hundred obituaries, numerous short stories, the novellas The Screaming House **and** Devil's Fork, **several novelettes, and the collections** Shadows of Appalachia **and** A Terrible Place and Other Flashes of Horror.

D.L. also serves as the President and Associate Editor of Undertaker Books, an independent horror publisher. In his spare time, he can be found searching for inspiration in the world around him and helping his wife try to keep their children from becoming the next generation of horror villains.

INDUSTRIAL DRIVE

BY A C HESSENAUER

INDUSTRIAL DRIVE

BY A.C. HESSENAUER

This is the story of the time a librarian saved my life. And I don't mean that in the way you're probably thinking. He didn't hand me a book that ended up meaning something so profound that it changed my life. No. I mean he legitimately saved my life, and he almost got eaten. It happened right here in town.

I grew up in a little town in Michigan called Livonia. No one ever knows where that is, so I got used to saying I grew up in the suburbs of Detroit. My neighborhood was known as "The State Streets," because—you guessed it—each street was named after a different state. I hailed from Maryland, and if you hopped on your bike and took Maryland to California, to West Chicago, out to Farmington Rd, one of the main roads in town, and you just kept going for a ways, you'd start to smell cinnamon.

That came from the bakery; Awrey's. We always joked that they must pump the scent of their cinnamon rolls baking out into the air to attract business. I drove past that factory practically every other day of my life, for years. It was a familiar part of life in Livonia. So was the surrounding industrial park.

The same exact businesses stood there for decades as far as I know. All with slightly technical sounding but non-impressionable names. Like

Sound Engineering, *Innovative Solutions*, or *Tub & Tile*. They were plain, boring, rectangular buildings, in drab beige and greys. The landscaping was always well-maintained. Neat rows of squarish shrubs sat out front with mulch beneath. The grass was always green in the summer. The sidewalks were shoveled in the winter. There was nothing odd or extraordinary about them. They were so mundane in fact, that your eyes tended to just skip over them as you drove past.

But here's the thing; I occasionally saw cars or delivery trucks in the Awrey's parking lot. People walking to and from their cars. But those other businesses? I never saw a single person leaving or entering a single one of them.

Another place that you can get to by taking Maryland to California, to West Chicago, to Farmington, was the Noble Library. My grandmother was a librarian, and had spent a few years at Noble, but by this time, the summer of 1999, she worked at the big library downtown, right next to City Hall. I used to walk into that shiny glass lobby absolutely beaming with pride whenever my mom took me to visit her at work. She ran the Children's Department, and made the most elaborate decorations by hand, pretty much out of nothing but construction paper and string. But I digress. Typically, I visited the Noble branch because it was much closer to home. So close that once I hit the age of 12, my parents let me ride my bike there all by myself.

Summers were always long and boring. This particular summer, my youngest sibling was born; a baby sister whom I adored. There was nearly a 13-year age gap between us, and my mom had my two younger brothers to take care of as well. I was rarely allowed play dates with my friends. With nothing to fill my days during the week, I would don my bright red backpack, ride my bike to the library, stuff it full of horror books (mostly Stephen King) and head back home to read the day away. A few days later I would be out of books again, and the same cycle would repeat.

One day, I was following the familiar aforementioned route out to Noble to get more books, when I felt an itch in the back of my mind. A sudden urge to keep going. I often spent several hours at the library, perusing the shelves. Sometimes I would curl up in a chair to read for a bit. My mother certainly wouldn't notice if I were to take a short detour. I paused in front of the library, deliberating.

Surely I was wrong. Surely, people did come and go in that industrial park. After all, we often drove past in the evening or on weekends. Surely if I went there during the day, and rode my bike past, I would see signs of activity.

I straightened the front wheel of my bike and pushed off before I could change my mind.

By the time I reached Awrey's Bakery it was probably around 10:30 in the morning. While I didn't see anyone around, there was a delivery truck idling in the parking lot, backed up against the loading dock. I breathed in deeply as I passed, the scent of warm cinnamon and vanilla causing my stomach to rumble.

Just past Awrey's was the *Sound Engineering* building. I slowed as I rode past. I caught a glimpse of a single white car in the back parking lot. I continued past the green street sign that read *'Industrial Drive,'* bouncing on my seat as the tires went over the crooked edge where the sidewalk met the road.

The next building was just as non-descript. Brown brick, a single line of shrubs out front. I stared at the windows as I rode past. No lights on in this building either. Unless the windows were tinted. The name out front spanned the width of the green awning, printed in white letters; *'Midwest Painting.'* I mulled that one over, my bike wobbling back and forth due to my lack of speed. Paint was bought and sold by the gallon at chain stores. I'd seen the walls of brightly colored swatches many times. Painters drove around in white vans, usually marked with their last name, *'& sons,'* and they probably didn't need a whole building with tinted windows.

I rode up the street a ways and turned around. I almost crossed over to the other side of Farmington to avoid being conspicuous, but there was no cross walk. My mom would be pissed if I got run over. The image of a dark, shadowy figure on the other side of the glass, watching me as I passed, sprung into my mind. Maybe the snooty male librarian at Noble was right; maybe I should be checking out books from the YA section, not adult horror.

I picked up the pace as I passed by the silent businesses on the way back, not taking another breath until I reached Awrey's once more, awash in the comforting scent of baked goods.

Those tinted windows bothered me. They stuck in my mind. I swapped books hastily that day in a rush to get home and regretted my choices. The next day, I was back on my bike, heading to the library.

When I entered, the cool AC air hit me like a wall. I strode past the bulletin board with flashy summer camp flyers, past the drinking fountain, and my gaze fell on the bank of computers in the center of the building. One older woman sat there squinting as she peered closer, working the mouse with one hand. The internet. Of course. Maybe those businesses did all of their, well … business, online these days.

I eyed the librarian's desk across from the checkout counter. It was him. Of course. He'd already spotted me, too. He was always kind, and I liked the way he dressed. Today he was wearing a little blue bowtie. But his clear judgement of my reading preferences irked me and made me feel slightly uncomfortable. My parents didn't seem to have a problem with me reading Stephen King, I didn't see why he should.

One of my favorite books to check out was written by *J.R. Salamanca*. It was called *Lilith*. I didn't fully understand it, but it was about a woman in a madhouse. The doctor who treats her falls in love with her as he starts to realize she might not be crazy after all. I felt a hot trickle of embarrassment when I recalled the librarian's expression the first time I checked it out. He was decidedly disappointed in me. I could practically hear him thinking, *"Where are her parents?"*

I moved towards the computers, and almost changed my mind, but he had caught me watching him and was already standing up and heading my way.

I explained what I wanted haltingly. I'd never asked to use the computers before.

He got me logged in and walked me through pulling up the internet browser. I noticed he chose the monitor that faced his desk directly.

He wore glasses, so I figured maybe he wouldn't be able to read what I was typing as I slowly pecked out the words with two fingers.

'Sound Engineering,' was the first prompt I tried.

This pulled up a seemingly random list. Lots of speakers and micro-phones for sale, all sorts of businesses with vague, similar sounding names.

None were an exact match. I added 'Farmington RD' next, and then 'Livonia' for good measure.

My efforts produced nothing helpful. I scanned the list of results for the logo on the building; curved lines radiating out in a sort of fan shape. Nothing. No business listing. No phone number to call.

I was stumped.

I tried the paint store next. 'Midwest Painting,' same thing.

That's when I really started to feel it. A funny tickle in my gut.

It was a bit familiar. I usually felt that when I stayed up late at night, reading with a flashlight under the covers.

But this was broad daylight. In a library, at noon on a Wednesday or a Thursday. And I was surrounded by adults. Still. I felt it. Hot and oddly foreign and familiar at the same time. Fear.

I turned to find the librarian peering over my shoulder. I logged off hastily, thanking him for his help as I ran for the doors. I remembered at the last second to leave my books on the return counter. I didn't bother to grab more.

I rode my bike past the entrance to the industrial park once more, scanning the buildings. Nothing had changed. There was a single car in the back parking lot of Sound Engineering. It looked like the same vehicle.

I turned around and made a slow second pass. The dark windows stared at me like lidless eyes.

The next day, in a rare change of events, my mom decided to take us all to the city pool. I think she probably regretted it about halfway through, as she sat perched at a picnic table under the large umbrella, bouncing my baby sister while she wailed. We didn't stay very long.

But still, I was tired and hot by the time we got home, and in no mood to head back outside. I regretted not checking out new books and I felt a tug to return to the industrial park. But I stayed inside and ended up playing with my brothers in the basement for a bit before I got bored. Then a new thought occurred to me.

When Mom was busy putting Sophie down for a nap, I snuck into the kitchen and found the distinctive thick yellow book that my parents kept lying around. I'd almost never seen them use it, but a new one came in the mail every so often, and Mom would throw the old one in the recycling.

I was feeling vaguely proud of myself, and a bit like *Encyclopedia Brown* as I scanned the list of 'S's' with one finger.

My heart jumped a little when I found it. 'Sound Engineering,' followed by an address on Farmington RD, then— '(734) 876-2555.'

My heart beat faster as I stared at the phone, tucked into its cradle on the wall by the fridge. I listened first for Mom's footsteps, but heard nothing. I lunged for the handset. My fingers moved clumsily, each key lighting up briefly as I depressed the number. I walked around the fridge, further into the kitchen, out of sight now, just in case she came down the stairs. The phone cord slapped against a cupboard.

I pressed the handset against my ear as the phone rang.

It rang four or five times. Just as I was about to hang up, a click rattled down the line and a woman's voice said cheerily, "Sound Engineering, how can I help you?"

"Uh ..." Some sort of strangled, garbled sound left my mouth. I wracked my brain for a response.

I recalled words my mother had used and blurted out, "Sorry! Must be the wrong number!"

I hung up hastily. I turned back to the Yellow Pages.

The entry for 'Midwest Painting' was there as well. I dialed the phone number.

The same exact cheery voice said, "Midwest Painting, how can I help you today?"

My heart leapt into my throat as I pictured her on the other end of the line, my brain conjuring the image of a 1940s receptionist, sitting in a dark, empty building behind tinted windows. Long painted nails like talons, blonde pin-up curls, and a smile frozen on her face.

There was an extended silence, then the voice said, "You're that little girl, aren't you? The one with the red backpack."

I slammed the phone into its cradle and ran to my room, hot tears of terror sluicing down my cheeks.

The following day was overcast. Cloudy, and cool. I knew as soon as my feet hit the driveway that it would rain soon.

I might have stayed home. I might have easily never returned to the industrial park again.

But I'd always wondered just what I would do if I were a character in one of the books I read. I thought I knew. I thought I could be brave, even when I was scared. That's the true definition of bravery, if you believed *Bastian Balthazar Bux*, which I whole-heartedly did.

So I went. This time I left my red backpack at home.

I stared at the dark windows as I rode past Sound Engineering. This time I turned to the left and ducked down Industrial Drive.

The same car was sitting in the back parking lot. White, slightly dirty, with a Chevy logo on the back. The license plate number read '000 000.' The parking lot was otherwise empty.

I continued down the street. The entrance to Industrial Drive was clearly visible at my back. I could see cars flying past down Farmington Road. Civilization was right there.

This was a normal street, in a normal, boring, Midwest suburban town. There was nothing special about Livonia. Our only claim to fame I'd ever heard was the label, "The Whitest City in America." My cheeks burned at the thought.

When I saw the gardener, I was deep in my own head. He stood there wearing a plain blue jumpsuit, a garden hose with a spray nozzle on the end held aloft. It was pointed at one of those non-descript squarish shrubs in front of a non-descript squarish building. I couldn't see the name of it from the sidewalk.

He was staring directly at me.

I was sure of it, as I continued down the sidewalk, his head slowly swiveling as he tracked my movements.

I looked away. *Pretend you don't see him. Pretend he's normal.*

I put the pedal to the metal and hightailed it up the road, which curved gently. A curve. That was all. I swear. I never even made a turn.

If I did, I have no memory of it now.

I don't wear a watch. I had no way to mark the passage of time, other than the sun in the sky. I don't know how long I rode through those winding streets, passing one boring building after another. Empty loading docks. Dark windows. Empty parking lots. I passed by a building that had three cars in the parking lot. I wondered how long it had been since they'd been moved.

A black sedan slowly ambled past me, a white businessman in a black suit at the wheel. His head was cranked to the left at an unnatural angle as he stared at me.

I kept going for a bit before turning around. I was afraid I'd find him waiting for me.

The street seemed to just keep going and going in both directions. I passed occasional side streets with bland-sounding names, each appearing practically identical to the last. More buildings with innocuous business names. How far did this complex go? I eyed the sun overhead with a panicky feeling and thought of one of my favorite *Stephen King* books that I had read recently; *The Girl Who Loved Tom Gordon.* My heart beat faster. But that wasn't my situation, was it? I was lost in the middle of the whitest city in America, not the middle of the woods.

He was standing in a parking lot now. The gardener from earlier. No hose this time. His arms were loose at his sides as he watched me ride past. The faint squeaking sound my pedals made as they rotated was starting to make me feel sick. I was getting thirsty, too. No backpack today. No water, no snacks. I had nothing with me.

I began to scan the business fronts. Maybe I'd spot a payphone.

Maybe in one of the lobbies.

No. I tried to imagine entering one of the buildings, but the thought of my hand on the door handle made me want to vomit.

I squinted overhead, attempting to check the position of the sun through the roiling grey cloud cover.

That was how you got out when you were lost, right? That was how she got out, in *Tom Gordon*. Was I remembering correctly? She followed the sun and figured out which direction was north.

But you didn't get lost. You didn't get turned around. You're still on the same street. It just doesn't end.

I stopped then. Listened. I could hear it. That low hum in the background. Cars flying past on Farmington. I couldn't be that far away. It had to be right around the next curve. Or the next.

What else can you do? I urged myself to think.

I've read so many horror books. There was a lesson in each one. People looked at me funny, when I told them I loved to read horror. They thought it meant I got some sort of sick kick out of being afraid, or reading about someone else suffering. But that wasn't it at all. It was all about learning. Surviving. Horror gives you hope. It lets you practice. Practice fighting monsters, practice *seeing* monsters, for what they really are. It can teach you what to do, and more importantly, what not to do.

There had to be something. Something I'd learned, in one of the stories I'd read, that would get me out of this mess.

It was too late for breadcrumbs. Too late for notes. My parents would have no idea where to look for me. As far as they knew, I never rode any further than the library.

Too late. Too late to go back and change anything. You can only go forward.

But was that true? I'd tried forward, and now backward, and neither of those worked.

I could try through.

I eyed the closest side street. Maybe there was a short cut. Another way out down one of these side roads. But I knew it. I knew deep down that the same thing would happen. That the road would stretch on and on before and behind me, and I would be trapped.

Trapped. Trapped.

So how do you escape? How do you escape when you're in the middle of a horror story? When it seems like there's no way out?

When I saw the white car, slightly dirty, with a license plate that read '000 000,' I felt a brief surge of hope. This was it. The back of Sound Engineering. I'd come to the end of Industrial Drive after all.

But my gaze swept past the squat building to Farmington Road, only to find it missing. Another building sat there instead. This one was grey and sprawling, with reflective, shiny windows, and it sat right where the main road should be.

I don't know how long I stood there, staring at the front door, but eventually, I climbed off my bike. I left it lying on the grass. There was only one way out of a horror story. I should know that better than anyone.

And that was through.

I had been wrong about it being dark inside the building, but I was pretty darn close on everything else.

A smiling blonde woman with a wavy bob sat behind the reception desk. The rows of cubicles to the left were all empty.

The first thought that popped into my brain was, *"My, what big teeth you have."*

Her white rows of chompers gleamed in the overly bright fluorescent lighting. She tilted her head to the side and motioned to a set of double doors to her right.

She continued to smile as she spoke, her red lips stretched too wide in a way that made her voice sound funny. "The only way out is through."

I didn't take my eyes off of her as I hurried past.

On the other side of the double doors was a long, plain, empty hallway that appeared to stretch endlessly before me. I followed it, heart hammering against my rib cage, recalling the old adage about mazes. I walked with my right arm aloft, my fingers brushing along the wall.

I took every right turn I came to. I seemed to walk for an hour at least before I came to another set of double doors, nearly identical to the first. I burst through them to find myself in an identical-looking empty corridor. Before too long, silent tears ran down my cheeks.

The next time I reached the double doors, I paused. I closed my eyes. When I opened them again, I stared pointedly at my right hand. I brought up my left hand and clapped them together.

My grandmother had taught me once that you could train your brain to break out of bad dreams by looking at your hands. In the middle of a nightmare, if you could control your hands enough to look down at them, and eventually to clap, then you could also learn to wake yourself up. I had tried it in more than one nightmare and this last time I actually brought myself out of it.

As I stared at my hands, I tried to imagine opening the door and walking out into the sunshine. But that would mean I was still stuck in the industrial park. I squeezed my eyes shut and pictured somewhere else instead. Somewhere familiar. Comforting.

This time, when the door swung open, the wall of freshly cooled AC air hit me in the face. My eyes went wide as I walked past the bulletin board advertising Y Camp and Sleep Away Camp at Bear Lake. I stopped at the drinking fountain. I was parched. I pressed the button and leaned forward, drinking from the cool stream tentatively at first, then in big gulps. The librarian behind the check-out desk gave me a funny look.

I ran to the desk and spoke in one breath, "I need your help. Can I use your phone? My bike—I-I need to call my mom."

She continued to type away, her nails clicking on the keyboard as she peered closer at the screen.

"Miss? I-I'm lost. I need help!"

Nothing. My stomach sank as I stared at her blank expression.

I spun to see the familiar librarian behind his desk, this time sporting a red bowtie. He didn't look at me. I walked over and cleared my throat. "Mister—" I realized I didn't actually know his name. "Sir, can you help me? I need to call my parents for a ride. I lost my bike."

He turned the page in the catalog he was thumbing through and sighed a little, running a hand through his short dark hair.

Oh God.

I'll spare you the details of how I screamed and cried and yelled. How I slammed my hands on his desk. How I ran to the front door and pulled and pulled on the handle. How it wouldn't open.

The sun was starting to sink lower in the sky, and I was trapped. Albeit in a more familiar place, but still trapped. I debated for a bit if maybe I had died. Was I a ghost, with no memory of my death? They did say that happened sometimes.

Eventually I wandered into the horror section, my feet following my typical route. I stood eyeing the familiar titles on the shelves. I grabbed the copy of *Tom Gordon* and held it in both hands. I opened it, letting the pages fall where they would, and took a deep inhale. The book even *smelled* real in my hand. My eyes went wide. *I drank water from the fountain …*

I walked to the end of the row and threw *Tom Gordon* as hard as I could at the far wall of VHS tapes. A good five or six of them fell to the ground. I stood there, waiting.

Footsteps. The librarian appeared. He stood there, frowning down at the mess. He crouched and picked up *Tom Gordon,* and held it in one hand, turning it back and forth. He looked around the little library, stared directly into the aisle I was standing in. With a frown still on his face, he walked back to the horror section, brushing past me, and placed the book back on the shelf. I watched as he searched up and down the aisles before returning to his desk. Then I got to work.

When I had everything ready, I grabbed *Tom Gordon* off the shelf once more and threw it at the VHS tapes.

This time he walked slower, his eyes wide as he surveyed the space.

When he reached the horror section, he came to a dead stop, his jaw going slack.

There on the floor, spelled out with all the Stephen King books I could find, I wrote 'HELP.' Right beneath the message, I left a single book. I watched as he knelt in front of it, and lifted it gingerly. His lips moved as he mouthed the title; *'Lilith.'*

His expression was grim as he looked up sharply and scanned the room. I followed as he rushed to the computer console table, sat at the monitor I had used the other day, and began to type furiously on the keyboard.

Yes.

The other librarian at the front desk had long since disappeared for the night.

I watched as he shut off the lights and headed for the door, keys jangling in his hand. Then he paused, turned back, and flipped the lights back on. He scanned the room one last time and was out the door in a flash, locking it behind him.

I waited. And I paced. And I cried again. How would he ever find me?

I pictured him pulling up in front of Sound Engineering. Maybe he would find my discarded bike in the grass out front. But even if he did; would he come inside?

I pictured the blonde receptionist lying to him with her lips pulled back to expose her teeth.

"No, there's been no little girl here. I don't know what you mean."

Worse, what if she did something to him? What if she hurt him? Was she even really human?

I stalked up and down the carpet. When the thought finally dawned on me, I kicked myself internally.

I had made the library appear as if by magic. Why couldn't I magic my way back to reception?

I approached the front door and performed the same trick again. The same steps, in the same order. This time I pictured the creepy front lobby.

When the door swung open, I stepped through automatically opening my eyes as I went.

She was standing in the middle of the lobby. Her back was to me, so I couldn't quite make out what was happening at first.

I heard it though. An odd sort of sound. The kind of sound you might make when you're chugging water, your throat bobbing as you swallow.

I approached cautiously from the side, and what I saw made my heart stutter. I was trembling before my mind could fully process it.

The receptionist had somehow unhinged her jaw like a snake, her features terribly stretched and distorted, as she swallowed the librarian whole. I took in his crisp pleated pants and shiny shoes. He let out a muffled scream.

There was an odd moment of stasis where my mind went completely blank.

Then I was at her desk, fumbling through the contents of her drawers. I tossed a stapler over my shoulder, knocking papers loose in my panic. I found a round glass paperweight and debated on braining her for a second. Then my gaze fell on a long, thin letter opener.

I didn't allow myself time to think.

I grasped the letter opener in my fist, cocked my arm back, and ran at her. I jabbed it into her temple, right behind her eyes as I screamed and screamed.

She let out a gagging, choking sound, and I watched in disgust, jumping back as she regurgitated the librarian. She reared back with an inhuman hissing shriek that made my bones turn to mush.

The librarian and I stared at each other in shock for a moment. He reached down and picked up his glasses that had clattered to the floor. Then he threw me over his shoulder and bolted for the door. I held my hands up in disgust. He was coated in some sort of thick, gooey substance. I nearly vomited over his shoulder as he pushed through the front door and sprinted out of the building.

He dropped me on the grass and sputtered, "Jesus Christ! What the *fuck* was that?"

I watched mutely as his chest heaved.

He stared at my bike, and then back at his car, parked at the curb. I grinned at the cars flying by down Farmington Road.

"Come on," he said, still gasping. "I'm going to give you a ride home. Hopefully your bike will fit in the trunk."

I managed to respond numbly, "If not, just leave it."

He nodded once, pushed his glasses back up the bridge of his nose, and grabbed my bike.

I don't really have a dollar to my name. My parents didn't really believe in giving us chores, but they also didn't believe in giving us an allowance. I wanted to buy him a gift. Something to say thank you, but there was really nothing I could afford.

I figured he probably liked books though, given he was a librarian and all.

That's how I ended up writing this. I realized I still don't know his name. I never asked. Not while he was driving me home, thunder breaking finally overhead as it started to pour. Not when he waved goodbye, as I walked my bike up the driveway.

I was grounded for a week for being gone so long. I was so grateful to be home, I didn't complain at all.

When my mom finally let me ride my bike again, I brought this story with me. I handed it to him mutely, and he stared at me for a long time before he read it all straight through, right there, while I waited.

He sat there after. Seemed like he wasn't sure what to say. But then he looked up, and his eyes were a little misty, and he had a funny little smile. He handed the story back to me as he cleared his throat.

"Thank you," he said, his voice pitched low. "Thank you for sharing that with me. I think … I think you should keep it."

So I did.

Then he nodded towards the horror section and said, "We just got a new batch of books you might want to take a look at."

He winked as I backed away from the desk.

Now I check out whatever books I want and he never says a word.

Anyway, I think I might want to be a writer someday when I grow up. Or maybe I'll be a librarian.

A.C. Hessenauer describes herself as a writer of horror with gothic romance & weird girl lit vibes. A.C. has self-published five novels and one novella, including Dread House, Jumpers, *and* MANI-MAL. *A.C.'s next novel,* Going to the Six, *is set to be released in 2026 by Cemetery Dance. When she's not participating in macabre ceremonies dedicated to the eldritch horrors out in the woods, A.C. enjoys spending time with her family: her husband, two sons, and border collie named Maximus. She loves a good horror movie, and of course, getting swallowed whole by a good book.*

CHASM

ORIGINALLY PUBLISHED IN THE SUBURBAN NIGHTMARES ANTHOLOGY BY HELLBOUND BOOKS

BY BRYAN HOLM

CHASM

BY BRYAN HOLM

They had been drifting apart. Diane knew this, and she wondered if Eric felt it as well. A numbness had insinuated its way into their lives, building a wall between them. Still, it was a great dinner, and a great night overall. Eric had been putting in an effort lately, resurrecting date night on Saturdays. They were finally checking off the seemingly endless list of new restaurants around town. Diane appreciated the effort.

"Should we do another bottle?" Eric asked.

Diane looked at her empty wine glass, "It is really good."

"That's why we Ubered, right?"

Diane smiled, "Why not?"

Back home, Diane embraced Eric as he fumbled off his shoes in the back hallway. They made their way upstairs, losing items of clothing as they went. Afterwards, in the dark, Eric snoring next to her, the room spun around in a sickening lull, smothering her to sleep.

Diane dreamed of a dirt tunnel, enormous, dark, endless. She was crawling through it, frantic. The wet soil was cold and black, slivering deep beneath her fingernails. The oxygen in the oppressive space was evaporating, her breath ragged. Behind her, a dark shadow grew.

Diane awoke to bright sun and a pounding headache. As her eyes focused, the room was still spinning. Diane barely made it to the toilet. When she finished, Eric was behind her with a glass of water and stifled laughter.

"When's the last time you threw up?" Eric asked.

Diane snatched the water from him, pounded it down. "Sophomore year? Good God." Round two was suddenly upon her.

Diane finally made it back to bed, a lurching crawl. Eric started to sink beneath the sheets. Diane stopped him. "Blinds," she whispered.

"What?"

"Bright light."

Diane closed her eyes and grimaced dramatically, a hand over her eyes, like a vampire at dawn, before disappearing under the covers. Eric got out of bed and banished the sunshine from the bedroom. An hour later, their phones started going off. First Diane's, then Eric's, two calls in a row.

"Go away!" Diane pleaded with the ceiling.

Eric's phone rang again. Groaning, he leaned over, grabbed it. "Shit, it's my boss."

Eric sat up straight, answering it. "Sir? What do you mean? It's Sunday..." A long pause, Eric put his hand over the receiver, mouthing to her, "Your phone."

"What?"

"Your phone, the date," he hissed.

Diane fumbled for her phone while Eric stammered, "Sorry sir, My wife and I have a horrible case of food poisoning. I thought I sent you an email this morning. I can't make it in." Another pause. "Yes sir, I'll be there tomorrow no matter what."

On Diane's home screen, a text from her boss. *'Everything okay?'* She looked at the date. It was Monday. How was that possible? Her stomach dropped, a cold sweat on her neck. Eric was still stuttering. "Yes sir, won't happen again, see you tomorrow."

He hung up, and they sat in silence. The room spun again for Diane, but she wasn't sure it was the wine anymore. They went over it again and again. Did they both really just sleep for nearly 36 hours? Could they have been drugged? If so, why, and by whom?

They walked the house. Nothing was missing, nothing was misplaced, nothing out of the ordinary. The doors and windows were locked, their clothes from Saturday night still scattered across the floor. They both checked their call logs, messages, and emails. Only Eric had a missed call on Sunday, from a blocked number. They finally collapsed on the couch.

"We should see a doctor. Maybe I can get us in on a cancelation," Diane said.

Eric laughed, "I don't know if that's necessary."

"You need to be more disturbed by this. This isn't normal. We're missing an entire day."

"It's messed-up, no doubt about it, but we've both been really stressed out lately, right? We got way too drunk, and we slept for a long time. That's it. It's not that big of a deal."

Diane left the room, exasperated. That night, they went to bed in silence, a line drawn in the sand between them. Diane hated to do that, made a point of it never happening, but her frustration with Eric warranted it. How could he just blow this off? Just forget about it? This was typical of him, never deal with a problem, just bury it. The tension between them that had been smoothed over as of late, came rushing back. It was hours before Diane could fall asleep.

Diane was dreaming again, she found herself in the tunnel again. The passageway was smaller, the floor softer... muddier. Her arms were half-buried in the soil, she had trouble keeping her chin above the muck. Behind her, the shadow grew larger. Softly, a boy cried in the darkness. Diane twisted her head, peering into the inky depths. The shadow shot forward, consuming her, turning her world to midnight.

Diane awoke the next morning alone. Eric had left early for work without a word. After a long, hot shower, Diane made their bed. As she pulled the sheets over on Eric's side, she noticed a dark spot, the size of a dime. She scraped at it with a fingernail. Crimson flakes broke free from the sheet. She brushed away what looked like dried blood.

Diane rushed out of the house, late for work; a flurry of spilled coffee and dropped keys. Out of the corner of her eye, she caught sight of her elderly neighbor, Janet, shuffling down the street behind her ancient basset hound. Diane pretended not to notice, loading her laptop bag into the car.

"Diane, Diane!" Janet yelled.

"Shit." Diane finally turned around, her best fake smile on display, "Morning!"

This was Diane and Eric's first house, a modest starter home in a first-ring suburb. Diane didn't miss their cramped one-bedroom apartment in the city, but she did miss the people. She had no idea how cliquish and vindictive the suburbs could be until they moved to one. Every time she made it from the front door to her car without speaking to another person was a win in her book.

Janet approached her, ignoring any reasonable sense of personal space. Diane knew this meant she was about to be privy to some neighborhood gossip. Gossip, in Janet's case, likely meaning someone hadn't cut their lawn in two weeks. Diane leaned on her car, bracing herself.

"Can you believe what happened? In *our* neighborhood?" Janet asked.

"What happened now, Janet?"

"I wondered if you two were out of town! You were the only ones not standing in your front yard gawking. The Miller's boy, he's gone."

"Gone? What do you mean?"

Janet told her the whole sordid story. The Miller's son, Hunter, only five years old, went missing sometime Saturday night. When his parents awoke on Sunday morning, his bedroom was empty. There were no signs of a struggle, but a backdoor was left open. Mr. Miller insisted he locked it before going to bed. Janet was not convinced of this detail however, on account of his drinking problem. A drinking problem Diane was confident only existed in Janet's head.

"It was a circus, Diane. Cops all over the place, news crews, too. They're still out there." Diane looked past Janet, down the street. Sure enough, two news vans sat idling at the intersection. "I'm sure they'll want to interview you. Channel 5 interviewed me, and I gave them *tons* of useful information, and they didn't even air it!"

Diane did not have a productive day at work after that. She scoured the town's newspaper website, but it offered nothing in addition to what Janet had already told her. She texted a link to Eric, and it was an hour before he responded, '*sad.*' It took considerable willpower to keep Diane from flinging her phone against her cubicle wall in response.

That night, Eric cooked dinner, a peace offering, and they began speaking again. As Diane expected, he did not seem rattled at all by this new piece of information. He was even mystified by Diane's reaction to it. In his mind, there was simply no connection between the missing child and their missing day, even though they happened to overlap. Diane clutched her fork tightly to keep from screaming.

"Did you cut yourself?" Diane asked.

"What? Where?" Eric reached up, touching his face.

"There was blood on our sheets."

"Weird. Not that I know of." Eric got up and cleared the table. Diane continued to pick at her food.

That night, Diane was back in the passageway. The mud underneath her was a soup, and swimming in it were thick, cold nightcrawlers. The worms were in a frenzy, a slime-covered orgy. She twisted her body to see behind her, the walls of the tunnel pressing down on her. The shadow of a child crawled towards her, crying in the dark... piercing and overwhelming. She cupped her ears with her hands. Her brain was pulsating, a slithering pressure growing, pushing against her skull.

Worms spilled from her nose and mouth.

Diane woke up screaming, her sheets wet with sweat. She raced to the bathroom mirror, convinced the worms were still inside her head, a wet echo of the dream following her into the light. The sight of her normal self did little to calm her nerves. After an excruciatingly hot shower, she put on a pot of tea, and called in sick to work.

It was later that day when the smell came. It was subtle at first, and Diane mistook it for mustiness that could be remedied by opening the windows. Then the smell turned pungent and sour. A mouse had crawled under their front steps to die the previous winter, and Eric assumed that's what it was again. Diane was unsure. This smell was different, more multifarious.

Eric took a hose to the space underneath the front steps, sprayed some Lysol, and called it good. The next day, when Diane got home from work, the stench was nauseating, permeating the entire house. Eric was working late, so she took it upon herself to root out the source. Armed with a flashlight, she ruled out the front steps, and made her way through every room of the house. As she approached the basement door, the smell became overwhelming.

Diane liked to call it their horror movie basement. She hated the wooden stairs that creaked with each step. She hated the cinderblock walls, covered in cobwebs and water stains that appeared every time it rained. She hated the single bare light bulb, which seemed to create more shadows than light. Most of all though, Diane hated the floor. There was no cement, only tight, packed earth.

The smell was overpowering in the small space. She had to choke down bile as she gingerly stepped onto the soil, sweeping the flashlight back and forth. In one corner were the rotting remnants of an antique firewood bin. Did something make a home in there? As the light pierced the darkness, something caught her eye. The dirt in the back corner seemed darker than the rest. Fresh, as if recently tilled.

Standing over it, it was indeed an inch higher than the earth around it. Diane tentatively pressed a shoe down on it. It was soft, loose. As soon as she disturbed the soil, another wave of the awful smell clamped down on her nostrils. Above her, the floorboards creaked. She almost dropped the flashlight.

Eric was home. He had picked up a pizza. As they ate, Diane told him what she had found. As she predicted, he didn't seem overly concerned.

"It's probably nothing," Eric said.

"You didn't do any work down there recently?"

"No. It's an old house, I'm sure the foundation just shifted a bit with all that rain last week."

"The smell is horrendous."

"You're too sensitive. I didn't smell anything when I got home."

Diane kept thinking about Eric's response as she washed up the dishes. He couldn't smell it? It was an outright lie, it had to be. It was still there, the stench, deep in her nose, clinging like bleach after a deep bathtub cleaning. Eric had agreed to take a closer look, but not until he returned home later that night. Diane had forgotten, he was meeting a college friend for drinks. He said he wouldn't be late, but he took an Uber rather than drive.

Diane sat on her front steps, scrolling through her phone, making her way through a bottle of white wine. Condensation rolled down the glass, a wet circle on the cement step beside her. It was a beautiful night outside, the humidity of the past few days had finally evaporated, and the rising chorus of insects seemed to agree. Children were playing in immaculately landscaped yards up and down the block. Dogs were barking from behind screen doors.

A car door shutting down the street broke her from her spell. Someone was leaving the Miller's house, another visitor in the endless parade of well-wishers. Diane felt a pang of guilt, she hadn't reached out to them in any way. She had gotten to know Hunter's mom, MaryAnn, in a neighborhood book club that had fizzled out after warring politics tore it apart. Diane wanted to stop over earlier in the week, but Eric had claimed to be too tired. The liquid courage warming her cheeks, she decided to get it over with.

Diane knocked on the door, carrying a basket she had hastily put together from odds and ends in the fridge, a bottle of wine, crackers, cheese. After a few seconds, she knelt to set the basket at the base of the door, planning a quick retreat. The door opened, and MaryAnn stood in the doorway, eyes puffy, looking shorter than Diane remembered, as if the weight of her current horror had already diminished her physically.

"I'm sorry. I know it's late, and you're probably exhausted," Diane said.

"No, thank you for stopping by."

Diane handed her the basket. "I wish it was a lasagna, but I'm not much of a cook."

"This is great. We could use more wine around here."

MaryAnn's attempt at a joke nearly crushed Diane's heart. After an awkward hug, MaryAnn invited her inside. Diane sat on the couch and listened to MaryAnn tell her story. Most of it she already knew from the news, but the thought of any silence between them terrified her, so she kept asking questions. Their son had simply vanished, and there were still no leads. No evidence of any kind and no suspects at all. Diane's eyes wandered to a framed photo of Hunter, posing with a baseball bat, a giant smile on his face, two front teeth missing. MaryAnn followed her eyes. "This summer was his first year in T-ball."

"It's an adorable photo," Diane replied.

"What am I going to do? It's been three days, and you know what they say about the first 48 hours..." MaryAnn faded into a quiet sob.

All Diane could say was how sorry she was. The silence she was dreading emerged, an unwanted guest sitting between them. Diane's insides twisted; her stomach lurched. The room suddenly felt off balance. A creeping nausea rose in her guts. "I'm sorry, but can I use your bathroom?"

Diane stood at the sink, her face gaunt under the harsh light. She splashed cold water on her cheeks, hoping to avoid vomiting in their house. What was wrong with her? She didn't have that much to drink. After several deep breaths, she dried herself off with a towel, still wet and slightly musty from the steady traffic through the house.

As she headed back to the living room, she passed Hunter's bedroom. The door was slightly ajar. Before she knew what she was doing, she was standing inside, surrounded by sports posters, toy cars, everything you would expect to see in a young boy's room. The silence of it felt like a tomb. Diane had a vision of this room, exactly the same, years later, covered in dust, a fading memorial for a vanished son. On a dresser was a worn baseball mitt. Diane reached for it. As she turned it over in her hand, she was struck by the familiarity of it. The leather was dyed black and red, in alternating stripes. Where had she seen it before?

"That was so nice of Eric." MaryAnn was right behind her. Diane jumped, her heart racing. She almost dropped the glove on the floor.

"I'm sorry, I don't know why I came in here."

"It's okay!" MaryAnn placed a hand on Diane's shoulder.

"What do you mean, Eric?"

"He was walking by one night, and Hunter was in tears because he had left his mitt at the little league field. When we had gone back for it, somebody had already taken it. Anyway, later that night, I heard Hunter talking to someone on the front porch. I found Eric, on a knee, laughing with Hunter. He had gifted him his childhood glove!"

"I didn't know about that."

"It was really sweet of him, and Hunter was elated!"

Diane imagined that scene in her head as she lay in bed that night. Eric still wasn't home, hadn't even texted a pre-emptive apology for being out all night. The interaction with Hunter seemed so out of character for him. He was always awkward around children. When they occasionally had to babysit her niece, he came up with every excuse imaginable to leave the house. Neither of them had ever wanted kids. It was something they had bonded over early in their relationship. Why did he not tell her about it? The noxious smell hit her again as she sunk into her mattress and she pulled the sheet over her nose.

Diane kept sinking as she fell asleep, back into the tunnel. The shaft was even smaller now, and the passageway felt much longer, a limitless space ahead of her in the darkness. It was so tight her arms were pinned to her sides. A wave of rot enveloped her from behind, along with a child's cry, even more distraught now, more panicked.

"Hunter?" Diane asked in the dark.

There was only deep silence in response. Then, small, cold hands gripped her bare feet. Diane tried to squirm forward, but the fingers dug in, impossibly strong, the tiny fingernails gouging the flesh around her ankles. Diane screamed but could not break free.

Diane awoke, gasping. She was sitting on the floor of the basement. Her hands were full of dirt, black soil caked under her fingernails. Her ankles were scratched and bloody. The smell was even more foul, alive. She fled up the stairs. Eric was in bed, snoring, undisturbed. Diane scrubbed her hands and ankles clean in the bathroom, then slipped into bed beside him. She could smell the liquor oozing from his pores. Diane knew sleep was off the table for the rest of the night.

Diane spent her workday stifling yawns and downing black coffee. She was tired, cranky, and a little behind, and she was afraid it was being noticed. She hoped hiding at her desk would do the trick, at least for one more day. Eric had woken up late of course, and they exchanged less than a dozen words as he scrambled out the door, a loose tie around his neck.

Eric had to work late again that night. Diane texted him that she was taking a valium and lying down. She included a friendly reminder that the basement smell was worse than ever, and could he please find a solution. Diane justified self-medicating because of her recent lack of sleep, but deep down she knew she was trying to avoid another night in the tunnel. The pill worked, along with two glasses of wine, and she slept soundly, dreamlessly.

The front door shutting woke her up. Still in a Diazepam fog, she checked the clock, it was three in the morning. Eric was not beside her. She crept to the window and looked out just in time to see Eric close the trunk of his car. He got in and drove away.

Diane made her way downstairs. Her head felt heavy, a slight wobble in her step. The door to the basement stood open, faint light filtering up the stairs from below. Diane made her way down, one hand on the wall for support. As she reached the bottom, she realized the smell was gone. In the corner, a hole had been dug, a shovel laid against the wall.

Diane couldn't see anything inside the hollow, only darkness. She stood at the edge, waiting for her eyes to adjust. The hairs on the back of her neck stood up, a cold trickle of fear moving through her chest. She was being watched; she was sure of it. A shadow moved inside the hole. Something was in it, breathing. Diane leaned closer. A child's hand shot out, pale and bloody. It gripped the edge of the opening, digging into the soil. Another hand joined it, feeling for something to hold onto. Diane fell backwards, hitting the floor hard. Everything went dark.

Diane awoke on the living room couch, a blanket over her. As she sat up, Eric came in, carrying a cup of hot tea. "Are you okay? You scared me."

"What happened?"

"You tell me. I found you in the basement passed out. Wasn't sure if I should call 911."

"I'm okay. I think. Just a bad headache."

"You shouldn't take those pills anymore. They really do a number on you."

Diane nursed the tea he brought her, tried to clear her head, remember what happened. She asked Eric where he had gone in the middle of the night.

"You were right, about the smell coming from the basement." Eric replied. "Craziest thing. I found a dead raccoon down there. Must have dug itself under, looking for a place to die."

"A raccoon? How did it get in?"

"I found a hole up in the rafters. Chewed right through the insulation."

"Where did you go?"

"It stunk so bad, I drove over to the park off Vernon, dumped it in the woods."

Diane sipped more tea. It tasted different; she couldn't quite place the flavor. She felt herself growing tired, her headache worsening. Eric helped her up to their bedroom. As she laid in bed, she felt the room tilt again, off kilter. She was sure she wouldn't sleep, but within seconds she was out.

Diane yawned and stretched in the morning sunlight. She glanced at her alarm clock. It was after ten. Diane bolted upright. She was late for work again, and Eric was gone. Why hadn't he made sure she was awake? Or at least set her alarm? Her phone wasn't on the nightstand. She made her way through the house, finding it on the kitchen counter, nearly dead.

On her home screen were dozens of texts and missed calls from her boss. *'Where are you?' 'Are you okay?' 'We need to talk.'* Diane's heart raced. She checked the date, but she already knew what it would say. It was Thursday, and it had been Tuesday night when she had collapsed in the basement. She was missing another day.

Diane called Eric. Waiting for him to answer, she realized her hands were filthy, dirt caked under her nails again. She held the phone between her neck and shoulder and scrubbed her hands in the sink. Diane turned off the water. Eric's ring tone was playing faintly, somewhere in the house. Diane redialed his number, following the sound.

She found Eric's phone lying in the center of the basement floor. His home screen echoed her own, missed calls and texts from an irate boss. She entered his passcode to see more, but it was rejected. She tried again and was warned she would be locked out. When did he change it? Eric's car was still in the driveway, his keys in the front hall. Diane grabbed them, slipped on her shoes, and went outside.

It was a brisk morning, a warning that fall was around the corner. Dread filled Diane as she approached the car. What was she scared of? What did she expect to find? Diane pressed the fob and popped the trunk. She stood there for a full minute, the trunk ajar, before opening it. The familiar smell hit her before dispersing into the morning air. The trunk was empty except for a crumpled blue tarp and a shovel. Diane leaned in closer. There were spots of dried blood on the shovel, a few brown hairs. Diane shut the trunk and went inside.

Diane sat on the couch, contemplating calling the police. What would she even say? She knew they would tell her she jumped the gun. That her husband would probably show up in a day or two with a bad hangover. Instead, Diane retreated to the kitchen and opened a bottle of wine. She went to bed alone that night, tripping as she crept up the stairs. The bottle of wine had not lasted long. As she fell into bed, she prayed she was too drunk to dream.

Her prayers went unanswered.

The tunnel was freezing, her ragged breath a cloud before her. Her arms were pinned against the tunnel walls. She rocked back and forth, kicking her feet. Diane slowly shimmied ahead, inch by inch. Her body shook from the cold, the mud like ice against her skin. A wind rose, hitting her in the face. She stopped, her heart pounding in her chest. The crying came soon after, like she knew it would, but this time it was ahead of her. She fought back tears, peering into the darkness.

"Hunter, is that you?" Diane pleaded. "I... I don't know what you want, but I'm not going to hurt you. I want to help you."

The crying stopped. Diane felt dizzy. She took rapid breaths, unable to find oxygen. Hunter slowly crawled out of the darkness toward her, his face pearly white, his cheeks sunken, bloodless. Diane screamed as his pale hands clawed at her face. His long fingernails gouged her cheeks, digging in. His mouth opened impossibly wide, his throat a shadowy abyss.

Diane woke up choking, gasping for breath. She was lying in the hole in the basement, her mouth filled with wet dirt. Screaming, she pulled herself out and sprinted up the stairs, vomiting in the kitchen sink, rinsing out her mouth with water. Her cheeks were on fire, cut to shreds, blood dripping down her neck. Diane's hands were bloody, chunks of skin deep under her fingernails. Diane threw up again.

The days merged together after that. Diane didn't leave the house, didn't answer her phone, letting it go dead on the counter. Her days were fueled by caffeine to stay awake, and her evenings were fueled by copious amounts of alcohol to stave off the night terrors. It didn't work. She wasn't even sure if she was awake or dreaming anymore, and she wasn't sure if she had lost any more days. She was too scared to keep track.

Diane was hunched over her kitchen sink, rubbing her temples, waiting for her coffee to brew when the smell returned. The odor grew throughout the day, becoming unbearable, even worse than before. It was everywhere, invading her clothes, her skin, her hair. She could taste it when she swallowed. The dark urine she left in the toilet smelled like it. She flushed three times to be sure it was gone.

By nightfall, she had finally drunk enough whiskey to face it. Diane crept down the basement steps, a shovel in hand. Each step down was a horrendous assault to her senses. She coughed and gagged as she stepped onto the dirt floor.

Diane began to dig.

Inches turned to feet; minutes turned to hours. Diane kept digging, a heap of dirt next to the hole. The dirt was alive; worms, centipedes, severed roots bleeding green. Diane was soon covered in mud, a mixture of soil and sweat. The mud was soon joined by blood, her palms splitting from the punishing work.

The smell kept getting worse and worse, as if she was mere inches from uncovering something ghastly and rotten, but it never materialized. Diane knew it had to be there, somewhere in that cursed basement, just out of her reach. As she struggled lifting a shovel full of dirt high over her head, Diane realized that she was probably too weak to climb out of the hole. She was several feet below the surface, and hadn't eaten anything in a long time. Instead of terrifying her, it only hardened her resolve. She dug deeper and deeper, at a furious pace, her hands ragged and raw.

Diane stopped to catch her breath, leaning on the shovel. A cold draft hit her neck, chilling the filthy sweat running down her back. A small portion of the muddy wall had collapsed, revealing an opening at the bottom of the pit.

Diane knelt in the dirt. It was freezing, her breath a cloud in front of her. It was a small tunnel, its clay membrane crisscrossed with tree roots. Diane leaned forward, peering into the darkness. The smell coming from it was overwhelming.

Diane crawled inside, shimmying into the skintight passageway. Behind her, the walls of the hole began collapsing, a chain reaction of tiny dirt avalanches filling the grave she had dug for herself. Darkness soon enveloped her, the oxygen vanishing rapidly.

"Hello?"

There was no reply, but Diane felt Hunter in the tunnel with her. She felt his soft breath on her face, his small, icy hands reaching out for her in the dark.

Diane closed her eyes for the last time, ready to embrace him.

Bryan Holm grew up in Minnesota and lives there with his wife and dog. He is a photographer by day who spends his nights writing and consuming all things horror. His short fiction has been published in anthologies by Sinister Smile Press, Eerie River Publishing, Strange Wilds Press, and Dead Sky Publishing. He was featured on the Bloodlist as a Fresh Blood Selects for his screenwriting. His debut novella, Satanic Static, was released by Anuci Press in 2025.

MEADOW GARDENS

BY EVE L FELL

MEADOW GARDENS

BY EVE L. FELL

"Did you go by the Clubhouse and register us yet?" My doting husband Riley yelled at me. I roll my eyes, dreading the fake smiles and laughs I will have to hand out like candy in front of the stepford wives of Meadow Gardens. It wasn't my idea to move to the suburbs in the first place. I don't think they particularly like women who have their own brain. "Honey, did you hear me? They'll be closing soon, it's already starting to get dark."

"Yes babe. I'll head that way now. I'll probably walk so I can get some fresh air and check out the neighborhood," I holler up the stairs at him. He comes to the top of the stairs and looks down at me just before I reach the front door. I smile at him as he blows a kiss and pretends to throw it my way. I catch it and put it in my pocket, blowing one back.

"Be safe, babe," he says before I step outside.

"I will, love you babe," I close the door behind me. Watching him disappear from my vision. How unsafe can the suburbs be, anyways? We worked our asses off to live in this specific upscale cookie-cutter neighborhood.

As I make my way two minutes to the Clubhouse, I take in all the identical houses, each a slightly different color to differentiate people's personalities I guess. The sun starts setting faster than I thought it would, but that's fall for you.

I see the Clubhouse come into view and it looks like all the lights are out. I check my watch and it says five-fourty. They don't close until six. Weird. Maybe they closed early. I think about turning around and going home, but I don't want Riley to be upset that I didn't get us registered before Halloween. In this neighborhood, to hand out candy you have to be registered with the homeowners association and the Clubhouse. I don't know many neighborhoods that make you become a part of the community Clubhouse, too. But this is what Riley wants, so this is what he will get.

I go to the front door and wiggle the handle finding it unlocked. I walk in and there's no one sitting at the front desk. "Hello? I'm here to register myself and my husband," I say in a louder voice trying not to yell and sound rude. I don't hear anyone answer. I do hear some kind of weird music and I decide to follow it, hoping to find someone to help me.

As I make my way down a hallway, the music gets louder and I don't recognize the genre of music that's playing. One thing I do know is it damn sure doesn't sound like something rich suburban housewives listen to. I take a couple turns trying to hone in on where the music is playing from and come upon two glass French doors. There is a baby blue curtain separating me from seeing what's happening in the room.

The music is so loud now I feel it reverberating inside my chest. I begin to sweat, hearing the lyrics clearly now, I realize the person is speaking in Latin. I also hear a group of women chanting with the music. I start to reach towards the curtain, my curiosity winning over fear.

As I pull a small part of the curtain back, what I see makes no sense inside my brain. My mouth drops open as I watch a housewife dressed like something from the 1950s, raise a giant blade above her head and continue to chant with the music. I strain to look around her. She is standing in front of some sort of table. There is plastic covering the floor around her. My hands feel clammy. She finally moves to the side and I catch a glance of a man. He is in ratty clothing and looks like he might be homeless.

The man is saying something, but I can't hear him over the music and chanting. Moral dilemma and anxiety swell up in my chest. Do I bust in here and try to save him, or is this some sort of fake show they do for shits and giggles around Halloween, or do I watch to see what happens and possibly see some crazy housewives murder a homeless man. I choose the latter, scared for my own safety. There are at least thirty women in that room all chanting. Even though I'm in shape and most likely stronger than one housewife, maybe even two. I'm not stronger than thirty.

I get my phone out with the intention of calling 911, but my phone is dead. I remember charging it. This is not fucking happening. I look back into the room just in time to watch the knife wielding housewife sink the giant hunting knife directly into the homeless man's chest and unbeknownst to me, I scream. Every single housewife in the room turns towards the French doors.

"Who in the world was that?" The main housewife says and no one says anything. I feel frozen like I can't move. I know I need to run. I've got to get home to Riley and warn him. We moved to the wrong fucking suburbs. "Well someone go look. NOW." She yells the last word and several housewives begin moving towards me and the French doors.

Suddenly I get control over my body again, and I dash away from the door as fast as I can. I try to make my way back through the hallways trying every door that leads to outside, each one locked. I hear several footsteps running behind me. I don't look in fear that they'll be right behind me and snatch me up.

I finally find the front door and trip over the door seal running outside. As I stumble and catch myself with my hands, I look forward and see nine pairs of heels. Each a different color. Each a different housewife. I slowly stand up straight and the one in the middle of them is holding the same hunting knife I watched her plunge into that homeless man's chest. It's still dripping with his blood creating a small pool at her feet.

I look to my left and right looking for emptiness to run into. To my horror, all sides of me are surrounded by housewives. All in their own perfect matching outfit, headband and heels. All holding weapons. I don't know what I've stumbled upon, but I have got to figure out a way to get the fuck away from them.

I open my mouth to scream for help, "Don't you dare open your mouth. Or I'll slice your throat open, right here in the parking lot. Besides, there is no one here who's going to help you." I shut my eyresquickly and I feel tears streaming down my face. Twenty minutes ago I was happy and excited about living in the suburbs with my husband, now I'm not sure I'm going to be alive in the next twenty minutes.

"Please, I won't say anything to anyone. Just let me go. We'll leave and never come back." I beg the main housewife. The one who looks to be the leader. I jump as they all start cackling loudly together in unison. I feel like I can't breathe as I look around at all of them.

"You're not going anywhere. You'll either join us or die," The leader says. I look at her and I could swear her skin is illuminated from underneath.

"Join you? What do you mean join you, is this a fucking cult or something?" I ask her as I look at all of them. Once again they all cackle together in unison. My blood runs cold knowing I'm not getting out of here alive. There are no other people out, no cars driving by, no people walking, and no one here to help. Just like she said.

I collapse to the ground giving up. I sink my face into my hands crying. All I wanted was to give Riley everything he ever wanted. To live in suburbia and live happily ever after with my own little family.

"You can still do that," I hear one of them say. I raise my head up with confusion written all over my face. How the fuck does she know what I'm thinking?

"It's a part of the gift Satan has given me. All he wants in return is new fresh recruits and blood. We all got a special gift from him. I just gave him his sacrifice for the month, now I need a new recruit. That's why you're here to register, right?" She tilts her head and looks at me waiting.

"What? I mean yes, but to register with the clubhouse and home owners association. I think we're far beyond that. I just watched you kill some homeless man." I laugh erratically, feeling like I'm in the twilight zone.

"Oh, you mean the homeless man your husband Riley delivered to us last night. The same homeless man that was sacrificed in exchange for us giving you a chance to join us?" I get up off the ground and I get into her face. She doesn't flinch.

"My husband would never do that!" I scream at her and back up just a tad, remembering the giant knife she's holding. "He's a good man." I say a bit softer.

"Sarah, join them please. This is what I want." I jump at the sound of my husband's voice and turn around to find him standing behind me.

"What?" I whisper as I feel the tears welling up in my eyes once more. "Riley, did you do what she said? Did you kidnap a homeless man and bring him here to be sacrificed, I-"

"Yes," He cuts me off before I can finish my sentence. "I sure did. I told you I wanted to live in suburbia and enjoy everything it has to offer. The women in my family have been doing this for a long time. I want you to continue the tradition."

"What tradition? Sacrificing homeless people t...t...to the devil, for what?" I yell louder than I intended.

"For stability and a self-sufficient community. We have everything we need in this suburbia. Our own grocery, our own farm, our own schools, our own hospital and our own little world. Once you pierce the bubble there is no returning to the normal world. We exist in here safe from wars, criminals, murder, rape, sickness and any other danger that threatens our wellbeing. We sacrifice one homeless drug addicted person a month and in return *he* provides."

I stare at my husband, the man that I love more than anything in this world, with my jaw dropped open, confused. I have no family left. My parents are dead. I don't speak to my extended family because my parents were the black sheep in their families. Riley is all I have. He walks up to me, closes my mouth and tucks my hair behind my ear. He plants a gentle kiss on my forehead and smiles at me warmly.

"Just say yes, Sarah. Everything we've ever wanted is here in Meadow Gardens. We'll live here forever and have our happily ever after. There is no death when you give yourself to *him*." He still has a gentle hold on my arms and I feel conflicted. He is my everything. I just don't know if I can kill an innocent human being every month for eternity. aAnd for what? For a safe, predictable and predetermined life?

"Yes, for exactly that. *He'll* begin your recruitment the moment you say yes," The leader of the housewives says behind me. I don't turn around and look at her or any of the other women. I just stare into my husband's eyes and see nothing but truth hiding there. He rubs my arms as he smiles once more.

I know I either follow my husband into the flames of hell in the form of suburbia or I will perish right here under his gaze. "Okay. If this is what you want Riley. I say yes," I say softly and look down at my husband's black designer loafers, wondering if this is the last time I will see them.

I feel hundreds hands painfully grab me at once and I'm thrown far into the air, landing on nothing visible. I'm floating, suspended in the air above all the wives, the neighborhood and my husband. Able to see everything and everyone, I look at the neighborhood and see it breathing beneath me. As I watch the houses take deep breaths in unison, I don't know if I'll ever be myself after whatever is going to transpire here. My new neighborhood, my husband and I in our forever home.. But as long as I'm with Riley, that's all that matters to me.

I look down at him and even from all the way up here I see him smiling. I see the love written all over his face. I know he's proud of me and my heart swells. If this is what it means to give myself to him, to these women, to this neighborhood, to *him,* that is what I will do.

The houses begin to breathe harder, the air gets hotter, a loud chanting fills my head and I feel my body start to tingle. I know my conversion is about to begin without being told. I watch with tears in my eyes and fear in my heart as something rises and tears through the ground of one of the cul de sacs.

The Devil.

Eve L. Fell was born, and still resides, in Kentucky. She tapped into her creativity at a young age, writing poems and short stories with the dream of being a successful writer. Eve tends to write on the darker side.

ANCHOR STORE

BY STUART CONOVER

ANCHOR STORE

BY STUART CONOVER

The mall was louder than it needed to be.

Music spilled out of storefronts in overlapping waves, each one trying to dominate the air. Synth-heavy pop from the clothing store bled into the thin guitar riff leaking from the record shop. Somewhere near the arcade, a machine screamed its electronic victory song again and again, the sound sharp enough to cut through the chatter of voices and footsteps.

David cut left without slowing.

He did not look back to see if the others followed. *He* never had to. *They* always did.

Matt nearly collided with a woman pushing a stroller and laughed as he spun out of the way, already jogging backward so he could keep talking. "We could shave at least two minutes if we cut past the arcade."

"It bottlenecks," David said. He reached up and adjusted the strap of his backpack, pulling it tighter against his shoulder. The motion was automatic. He always did that when he needed to focus. "Everyone does that."

"Everyone is slow," Matt said, grinning. He pivoted and sprinted ahead, weaving through a knot of teenagers clustered outside the music store. He doubled back again, breathing hard but energized, like the mall itself was something he could race.

Chris stayed close to the edge of the walkway, careful not to get swallowed by the crowd. His eyes moved constantly, not darting, just tracking. Store signs. Ceiling tiles. The repeating pattern of the floor. Where every single person was in front of him and what direction and speed they were moving in.

He frowned and slowed.

"They moved the directory," he said.

"No, they didn't," Matt called from somewhere ahead.

"They did," Chris said, more to David than to Matt. "It used to be by the fountain. Now it's closer to the shoe store."

Angela nodded without looking at him. She was already scanning the storefronts ahead, eyes flicking between window displays like she was cross-checking a list only she could see. "They rotated the kiosks too," she said. "That one used to sell candles. Now it's phone cases."

David slowed just enough to keep the group together. He did not ask how Angela knew that. She always knew things like that. The mall changed constantly, but she noticed it all.

"We cut through the north wing," David said. "We stay moving."

"Always stay moving," Matt said, suddenly solemn. "Mall rule number one."

"That is not a rule," Angela said.

"It should be."

They passed the newly reopened anchor store without looking at it.

Everyone did. It had been closed for far too long. While some strolled in, there wasn't any real buzz, and just as many people avoided the entrance altogether.

Its wide entrance was sealed with a metal gate pulled down tight, the lights off behind it. The space it occupied felt heavier than the other stores, not darker exactly, just absent. People unconsciously shifted their paths around it, angling slightly left or right without ever seeming to notice they had done so.

Chris felt the familiar prickle at the back of his neck as they passed it, the sense that there was something he should be paying attention to. He did not stop. He never stopped the group unless he was sure.

Ahead of them, a lone figure moved against the flow of traffic.

The uniform was pale and indistinct. Janitor, maybe. Security. Mall employee. The kind of person you trusted without thinking about it.

"He knows where he's going," Matt said, already angling toward him.

The figure did not look back. He moved with easy confidence, slipping between clusters of shoppers without breaking stride, never bumping into anyone.

David hesitated for half a second.

Chris noticed immediately, "That hallway doesn't go anywhere," he said. "It's service access."

"It goes somewhere," Matt said. "Watch."

The figure turned down a narrow corridor tucked between two stores. No sign marked it. No gate blocked it. Just a gap most people ignored because it did not promise anything.

Angela's eyes lit up. "Shortcut," she said, like she had just been proven right.

David made the call.

"Fine," he said, and waved them on.

The noise dropped off almost immediately.

The music faded first, then the layered sound of voices thinned until it felt like someone had turned down a dial. The lights buzzed louder here, fluorescent and flat. The carpet under their shoes felt thicker, softer, like it had been laid over something uneven.

Matt slowed, just a little. "This feels weird."

"It's fine," David said. "Just keep moving."

The hallway curved gently to the right. The figure stayed just ahead of them, always visible, never close enough to reach.

Chris glanced back.

The mall entrance behind them felt farther away than it should have been. The sound of the crowd was gone completely.

The hallway opened suddenly.

They stepped through a wide threshold, and the air changed.

They were inside the anchor store.

For a moment, none of them moved.

The air inside the store felt different, cooler but not cold, like it had been sealed off from the rest of the mall for a long time. The smell was faint and difficult to place. Clean fabric. Cardboard. Something older beneath it all, the way storage rooms smelled when boxes had not been touched in years.

Matt broke the silence first "Okay," he said quietly. "This is weird."

David nodded "We'll find the exit. We just came in the wrong way."

He said it like a decision, not the complete stab in the dark that it was.

They took a few careful steps forward. The music overhead drifted through the space in a slow loop, a pop song stretched thin enough that the melody never quite became clear enough to make out the lyrics. The speaker system must not be set up properly yet. It made it hard to tell how much time was passing. Each note seemed to linger a little longer than it should have.

Angela ran her fingers lightly along the edge of a display table as they passed. "Everything's set so perfectly," she said. "Perfectly. No clearance tags. No sale signs."

"Well, they only just reopened; it'd be hard to run a sale with everything being brand new," Matt said, though his voice lacked conviction. He craned his neck, trying to see over the tops of the shelves. "There has to be a front desk somewhere."

Chris stayed close to where he thought the entrance should have been. He turned slowly, trying to line up what he was seeing with what he knew of the mall's layout. The shelves were too tall. The aisles were too long. The ceiling felt higher than it should be.

After a few minutes of walking, Chris stopped and sputtered out, "This store is too big."

David looked at him. "What do you mean?"

"Yeah, this place is supposed to be huge," Chris said. "I know that. But this goes farther. We should be under the parking lot by now."

Matt laughed, sharp and quick, "You do not know that."

"I do," Chris said. "I counted the steps once."

Angela glanced at him, "Why?"

He shrugged, "I was bored."

They walked deeper into the store.

Shoppers moved around them without acknowledgment, pushing carts filled with carefully arranged items. Towels folded into perfect rectangles. Lamps boxed without logos. Clothing sorted by color instead of size. No one spoke. No one reached a register. No one appeared frustrated.

David felt a faint pressure behind his eyes, like the sensation of being watched without being seen.

Finally, ahead of them, a row of registers stood beneath bright lights. Each one was staffed by a cashier standing perfectly still, hands resting lightly on the counter. Their eyes were open. None of the machines were on.

A soft chime sounded somewhere to their left.

Chris flinched.

"Did you hear that?" he asked.

No one answered him right away.

They reached a wide intersection where signage hung from the ceiling. HOME. APPAREL. SEASONAL. The arrows pointed in every direction, each one identical down to the scuffed metal frame.

"All right," David said. "We pick one and stick to it."

"That one doesn't look right," Angela said, pointing toward SEASON-AL. "The lights are warmer."

Chris shook his head, "That does not mean anything."

"It might," Angela said.

They followed the SEASONAL aisle.

Artificial greenery filled the shelves. Cardboard boxes stacked high, each marked only with a number. No holiday branding. No decorations. Just materials waiting for a purpose that had not yet been assigned.

Chris counted his steps under his breath.

At forty-six, the aisle should have ended.

It did not.

Matt stopped abruptly. "Okay. That's new."

They stood at the intersection again.

The signage above them was exactly the same. Same arrows. Same scuff on the left corner. Same slight tilt in the frame.

"That's not possible," Matt said.

Angela stepped closer to one of the signs, "These are not signs," she said. "They are suggestions."

As if in response, one of the arrows creaked softly and shifted a fraction of an inch.

Matt took a step back, "Did that just move?"

David raised a hand, "Nobody panic."

Shoppers were closer now.

Not surrounding them. Just present. A man pushed a cart past the end of the aisle, then another. A woman turned smoothly into HOME, her cart wheels whispering against the polished floor.

Chris noticed something then. None of the shoppers crossed the intersection straight through. They all turned. Every single one of them.

"They do not want us going forward," he said quietly.

David exhaled, "Fire exits are usually near restrooms or stockrooms. That means back of house."

Chris pointed without hesitation, "That way."

David did not ask how he knew.

They moved together, choosing an aisle that narrowed as it went. The shelves closed in, rising higher, packed with items that felt increasingly specific.

A lamp identical to the one in David's living room.

A folded jacket that matched Matt's down to the frayed cuff near the wrist.

Angela slowed near a shelf of books. Their spines were blank. No titles. No authors.

Chris stopped completely.

"That," he said, his voice barely audible, "is my handwriting."

On the shelf sat a folded slip of paper, squared neatly with the edge. Beneath it rested a small white label with a number printed in thin black ink.

Angela leaned closer, "What is it?"

Chris swallowed., "It's a note. From the librarian. She wrote it for me."

Matt frowned, "I have never seen that."

"No one has," Chris said. "I kept it."

A throat cleared behind them.

It was the first human sound anyone else in the store had made.

"You will need to decide," the cashier said softly to Chris.

A soft chime sounded again.

At the far end of the aisle, an exit sign flickered to life.

Chris did not move. He couldn't.

-

The exit sign at the end of the aisle hummed softly.

Its red glow did not flicker now. It held steady, bright enough to draw the eye without demanding attention. It felt separate from the rest of the store, like it belonged to a different set of rules.

David stepped closer to Chris, "We do not have to do anything yet," he said. "We can figure this out."

Chris nodded, but his eyes never left the shelf.

The folded paper sat exactly where it had been placed. Neat. Squared. Cataloged. The small white label beneath it looked brighter now, as if the number had been freshly printed.

Angela leaned in, careful not to touch anything, "That label was not there before."

"Yes it was," Matt said automatically.

Angela shook her head, "No. It was not."

The cashier stood a few steps away, hands folded in front of them. They did not block the aisle. They did not hurry anyone along.

"You will need to decide," the cashier said again.

Matt exhaled sharply, "Decide what?"

The cashier's gaze did not leave Chris, "What you are willing to leave behind."

David turned on them, "That is not how this works. If this place wants something, it can take it from all of us."

The cashier looked at David for the first time.

Their expression was not hostile. It was almost curious.

"It does not want all of you," they said. "It only needs what was offered."

Matt laughed, a short sound that did not quite land. "Offered? Nobody offered anything."

Chris remembered the doorway.

The way the threshold had felt wrong to rush through. The instinct that had made him pause. The small, ordinary act of holding the door open so the others could pass first.

"I did," he said quietly.

Everyone looked at him.

"I was last," Chris continued. "I held the door."

The cashier inclined their head. Just a fraction. "That was considerate."

The word landed heavier than it should have.

Angela's voice was tight. "What happens if he does nothing?"

The cashier answered without hesitation, "Then you remain."

The shoppers drifted a little closer.

Not enough to touch. Not enough to block the aisle. Just enough to be present.

The music overhead softened, the notes stretching thinner, as if the store were listening.

David stepped in front of Chris without thinking, "Then take something from me."

The cashier shook their head, "It would not fit."

"Why him?" Matt demanded, "Why does it have to be him?"

The cashier considered this. "Because he noticed. Because he waited. Because he made space. And whatever he decides, will be gone."

Chris felt something settle in his chest.

Not fear.

No.

Recognition.

He reached out and lifted the folded paper from the shelf.

For a moment, nothing happened.

Then the music shifted.

The melody resolved slightly, the notes finding a pattern that felt almost complete.

Chris unfolded the note.

The handwriting was exactly as he remembered it. Neat. Careful. Famil-iar. Words of encouragement written for no one else to see. Words that had mattered because they had been private.

He did not read them.

He folded the paper again and placed it back on the shelf, aligning it carefully with the edge.

The label beneath it brightened.

The exit door clicked.

"You can go," the cashier said.

Matt stepped forward immediately, "We are not leaving him."

Chris shook his head, "I am coming with you."

Angela stared at him, "You will not even remember what that was."

Chris nodded, "I know."

David grabbed his sleeve, "This is not fair."

"No," Chris said. "But it works."

The cashier stepped aside.

The path to the exit was suddenly clear.

David hesitated for only a moment longer, then pulled Chris with him.

They ran.

The floor beneath their feet felt normal again. The air grew warmer with every step. The exit door swung open easily.

Chris crossed the threshold last.

Again.

-

They burst back into the noise.

The mall sound hit them all at once. Music layered over voices. Footsteps on tile. The sudden crash of a dropped tray somewhere near the food court, followed by laughter and shouted apologies. The brightness felt harsh after the muted light of the store, like stepping outside after a long movie.

Matt staggered and laughed too hard. "Okay. Okay. We are out."

David spun around immediately.

There was no door.

No fire exit. No glowing sign. Just a smooth stretch of beige wall between two stores, broken only by a poster advertising a summer sale. The paper was curling slightly at the corners, taped unevenly like it had been there for years.

"That is not possible," Angela said.

She stepped closer and pressed her palm against the wall. It was warm from the overhead lights. Solid. Ordinary.

David searched for any trace of what they had just come through. A seam. A vent. A mark on the floor. There was nothing.

Chris stood a step back from the others, breathing slowly. His chest felt light, like he had let out a breath he had been holding for a very long time.

They drew the attention of a few passing shoppers. A woman frowned at them, then looked away. A man stepped around them without slowing.

No one else saw anything wrong.

Matt dragged a hand through his hair, "Did we just come out of a wall?"

David did not answer. His eyes had lifted to the mall directory across the atrium.

The anchor store was listed again.

COMING SOON.

Angela followed his gaze. Her stomach tightened, "That was not there before."

"No," Chris said. "It was not."

They stood there longer than they should have, staring at the directory as if it might correct itself. It did not.

David exhaled, "We should go."

They started walking, folding back into the flow of people. The mall accepted them without hesitation, closing around them like water.

They passed a photo kiosk near the fountain.

Chris slowed.

He frowned at the display of framed pictures, then stepped closer. His eyes moved across the rows, searching for something he could not quite name.

"These used to be school photos," he said.

Matt glanced over, "So?"

"They were grouped by year," Chris said. "By grade."

Angela leaned in. The pictures were generic now. Smiling faces. Stock images. No names. No dates.

David turned to Chris, "What is wrong?"

Chris opened his mouth.

He closed it again.

"I had something," he said finally. "I used to carry it with me."

Matt tilted his head, "Like what?"

Chris tried to answer.

He pictured paper folded small enough to fit in his pocket. Writing he trusted. Words that had made him feel seen in a way he did not know how to explain.

The image slid away as soon as he reached for it.

"I'm not sure," he said.

Angela felt a chill creep up her arms. "Chris."

He shook his head, "It is gone."

David frowned, "You're shaken. That place messed with us."

Chris nodded because that explanation made sense.

It made sense to everyone.

They reached the mall doors and stepped out into the late afternoon sun. Heat pressed down on them, solid and real. Cars moved through the parking lot. Someone shouted across the asphalt. A radio played too loud from an open window.

Behind them, the mall stood exactly as it always had.

Inside, the anchor store waited.

-

Chris went to the library three days later.

He did not plan to. He had been walking home from school, turned down the wrong block without realizing it, and ended up there the way he often did when his thoughts needed somewhere to slow down.

The library doors opened with their familiar soft resistance. The smell inside was the same as it had always been. Paper. Dust. Something faintly sweet from the old wooden shelves.

The librarian looked up from the desk and smiled when she saw him.

"Hi, Chris," she said. "Finding everything you need?"

The question caught him off guard.

There was a brief, strange pause where he expected something else to follow it. A look of recognition that lingered too long. A comment about a book he had checked out. A reference to a conversation he half remembered having.

"Yes," he said instead. "I think so."

He moved through the stacks slowly, fingers brushing spines he knew by heart. Local history. Old maps. The reference section where the bindings were cracked from too many careful hands.

Everything was where it should have been.

Almost.

He stopped near the bulletin board by the reading tables.

A handwritten note was pinned there, curling slightly at the edges.

PLEASE RETURN ALL MATERIALS ON TIMETHANK YOU FOR HELPING KEEP THE LIBRARY RUNNING SMOOTHLY

The handwriting was neat. Careful. Familiar.

Chris stared at it longer than he meant to.

A pressure built behind his eyes, gentle but persistent, like a thought trying to form without words. He knew he had seen that handwriting before. He knew it had once mattered to him.

He could not remember why.

Behind him, the wheels of a book cart rattled softly as the librarian passed. She glanced at the board, then back at him.

"You always notice the little things," she said, not unkindly.

Chris turned, "I do?"

She smiled, "You do."

The pressure eased. Whatever he had almost remembered slipped away again, leaving behind a small, clean absence. Like a space on a shelf where something used to sit.

Chris checked out a book and walked home.

That evening, the mall directory was updated.

COMING SOON was replaced with a store name no one questioned, and no one recalled being unfamiliar. The letters were clean and evenly spaced. The listing looked like it had always been there.

The anchor store's lights came on for the first time.

Inside, shelves stood in perfect order. Shoppers moved through the aisles without hurry. Registers waited patiently.

On a quiet shelf near the back, a folded note remained carefully cataloged, squared with the edge, preserved.

The store did not rush.

It never did.

It would wait for the next person who noticed the wrong thing. The next person who held a door open a little too long.

Stuart Conover is a father, husband, rescue dog owner, horror author, blogger, journalist, horror enthusiast, comic book geek, science fiction junkie, and IT professional. With all of that to cram in on a daily basis, it is highly debatable that he ever is able to sleep, and rumors have him attached to an IV drip of caffeine to get through most days. A resident in the suburbs of Chicago (and once upon a time in the city), most of Stuart's fiction takes place in the Midwest, if not the Windy City itself. From downtown to the suburbs to the cornfields - the area is ripe for urban horror of all facets.